ALSO BY

DONATELLA DI PIETRANTONIO

A Girl Returned

A SISTER'S STORY

Donatella Di Pietrantonio

A SISTER'S STORY

Translated from the Italian
by Ann Goldstein

Europa
editions

Europa Editions
1 Penn Plaza, Suite 6282
New York, N.Y. 10019
www.europaeditions.com
info@europaeditions.com

Copyright © 2020 by Giulio Einaudi editore s.p.a., Torino
First Publication 2022 by Europa Editions

Translation by Ann Goldstein
Original title: *Borgo Sud*
Translation copyright © 2022 by Europa Editions

Library of Congress Cataloging in Publication Data is available
ISBN 978-1-60945-747-1

Di Pietrantonio, Donatella
A Sister's Story

Book design by Emanuele Ragnisco
www.mekkanografici.com

Cover illustration by Elisa Talentino

Prepress by Grafica Punto Print – Rome

Printed in Canada

For Paolo, for the strength you didn't know you had

I was twenty-five years old when I got married.
I had always wanted to get married but had often thought,
with a sense of gloomy resignation,
that there wasn't much prospect of its happening.
—NATALIA GINZBURG, *My Husband*
[tr. Paul Lewis]

A SISTER'S STORY

1.

The rain poured down on the celebration without any warning thunder; none of the guests had seen the clouds thicken above the darkly wooded hills. We were sitting at the long table on the lawn when the water began to hit us. We were eating *spaghetti alla chitarra*, and the bottles were already half empty. At the center of the embroidered tablecloth the crown of laurel that Piero had taken off after the pictures scented the air. At the first drops he looked at the sky and then at me, sitting next to him. He had taken off his jacket and tie, unbuttoned the neck of his shirt, and rolled up his sleeves to the elbows: his skin radiated health, splendor. He hadn't slept much, nor had I, with him, except toward morning. For a few moments upon waking I hadn't known who I was, whom I loved, or that it was the start of a happy day.

Piero looked at me, surprised by the bad weather. A hailstone splashed the wine in his glass. Some of the guests went on chewing, unsure what to do. My sister had already jumped to her feet, collected the oval platters with the leftover pasta, the baskets of bread, and put them safely in the kitchen on the ground floor. We took shelter under an awning, while Adriana continued to run between inside and out, assailed by the wind. She fought the storm for the food, she wasn't used to waste.

I was leaning out to take the last trays from her hands when part of the gutter collapsed, hitting me. Blood dripped from my wounded cheekbone onto my chest, mixing with the rainwater. For the occasion I had chosen a white dress. It looked good on me, Adriana had said that morning, it was a kind of tryout for a wedding dress. We had arrived early, to help with the preparations. From the window I'd seen the low silent flight of the swallows: they sensed the rain. But Piero's mother wasn't expecting it; she had insisted on celebrating the graduation at their country house.

I have a photograph of the two of us, in love, looking at each other, Piero with the laurel on his head, eyes of devotion. At the edge of the frame Adriana appears: she entered the shot at the last moment, and her image is blurry, her hair draws a brown wake. She has never been tactful, she interjects herself into everything that has to do with me as if it were also hers, including Piero. For her he wasn't very different from a brother, but nice. My sister is laughing blithely at the lens, ignorant of what was to come for us. I brought the photo on this trip: the three of us still young, enclosed in an inside pocket of my purse.

Years later Adriana and I found the dress among the clothes I no longer wore; a faint halo of blood remained on the material.

"That was a sign," she said, waving it in front of my face.

2.

I can't sleep in this hotel room. I give in to exhaustion, but wake quickly with a start, open my eyes in the darkness. It's a long time since then, and the celebration of Piero's graduation is an unreliable memory, or a fragmentary dream. I may not be able to re-establish the truth of anything, after the phone call I got yesterday. The dim light of the corridor filters under the door, along with a faint shuffling. Other memories pass by, crowding, disorderly. Memory chooses its cards from the deck, exchanges them, sometimes cheats.

I traveled all day, on various trains, listening to the loud-speaker announcements first in French and then in Italian. The names of the smaller stations, where we didn't stop, filed by in a flash; some I couldn't manage to read. Suddenly in the afternoon the window was filled by the sea, the rippling Adriatic, so close to the train tracks in some places. Crossing the Marche I had the optical illusion that the buildings were leaning toward the beach, as if drawn by the water. Adriana doesn't know I've arrived. I'll go and see her tomorrow, but not in Borgo Sud.

Here in the hotel they asked me if I wanted to eat, but I said I was too tired to come down to dinner. Strong, kind Abruzzo knocked while I was watching the news, brought me biscuits and warm milk in the hands of a fair-haired girl. I didn't add sugar: it was sweet without. The forgotten taste of our first nourishment: I drank it in small sips—I wasn't expecting all that comfort.

Christophe says that milk is bad for adults, that only man is so stupid as to go on drinking it after he's weaned. But then I saw him come out on the landing reaching into a bag of potato chips. He is my across-the-hall French neighbor, who works at the synchrotron in Grenoble. We share a cat and the care of some plants that live between our doors. I left him a note before departing; he'll have to look after them now.

But sometimes when Piero came home late in the evening, he liked it: "I'll just have milk and biscuits."

We always had them in many flavors, for breakfast. He'd dip them in the cup one by one, holding them between thumb and index finger, and tell me about the day.

The house we lived in as husband and wife isn't far from here. I mentally review the cross streets that divide this street from Via Zara. I still have an image of that apartment so precise that even today I could list every detail: the cracked tile in the bathroom that sounded mutely if you walked on it, the evolutions of the light on the walls in the daytime hours. The first wake-up for us was a faint rattle at the window when the sun came to warm it, a sudden expansion of the glass. Piero would start to turn over, protesting against the necessity of getting up. We breathed an air that was always faintly blue, coming from the balcony that looked out on the sea. The sea evaporated in our house.

Here there's no salt smell, and the sound of the waves barely filters in from outside.

I didn't sleep that night, either, in the bed that was too wide. It was our third summer there, the new smell of the furniture had disappeared, and in the kitchen the stove had lost its shine. Piero was looking after his father, who was in the hospital. At the darkest moment before dawn someone pressed the bell furiously. She shouted her name and in a moment was on my floor, breathing hard, her nervous steps arriving outside the door. I delayed a moment turning the key to unlock the door, on the other side she was grumbling at me. I hadn't seen her for more than a year: my sister.

As children we were inseparable, then we had learned to lose each other. She could leave me without news of herself for months, but it had never been this long. She seemed to obey a nomadic instinct; when a place no longer suited her, she abandoned it. Every so often our mother said to her: you're a Gypsy. Later I was, too, in another way.

She rushed in, and with a push of her foot backward closed the door behind her. One of the slip-ons she was wearing fell off and stayed on the floor upside down. The baby was sleeping in her arms, his bare legs inert along her thin body, his head under her chin. It was her son, and I didn't know he'd been born.

I couldn't have imagined the revolution that was about to begin: if I had foreseen it I might have left them outside. Adriana believed she was an angel with a sword, but she was a careless angel and sometimes wounded by mistake. If she hadn't arrived, who knows, maybe all the rest wouldn't have happened.

Our last encounter had ended in a quarrel; after several weeks I'd looked for her in vain. I was waiting for a move from her. None of our common acquaintances had seen her in the city, but now and then she'd send a postcard to our parents, up in the town. They showed them to me when I went to see them: port of Pescara, Pescara by night. Many greetings from your daughter, then the signature with a flourish. She knew that I would read them, they were for me: the proof that she was alive and nearby.

Her move came at three in the morning of a June day. I don't know how long I would have stood still and silent, looking at them. From the back like that the baby seemed a large doll, one of those his mother never had as a child.

I almost didn't recognize her: she was wearing a nearly shapeless straw hat, with faded fake flowers on the broad brim, the edge frayed on one side. Under it, however, the eyes were hers, luminous and sharp, but wide open, as when she was afraid.

She asked me about Piero, I told her where he was. Then she got impatient with both of us standing in the entrance, and almost went through me. She hadn't forgotten the house, where she'd been a few times, and headed confidently toward the bedroom. She put the baby on the bed and covered him with the sheet, then sat down next to him. I was in front of her and she didn't speak, she held her sweaty face in her hands, elbows on her knees. At her feet the bag she'd dropped from her shoulder.

"What happened?" I tried to ask.

She didn't answer, but went to the window to hide her tears. She was trembling slightly, her shoulder blades prominent under the nightgown that I had taken for a summer dress. The edge of the hat bumped against the glass and it fell off. Over her right ear a single snip of the scissors had cut her shoulder-length hair cleanly, as in a game of hairdresser with a bad ending. She immediately covered up the damage, ignoring the surprise on my face. A faint rustling, the baby had thrown off the sheet and turned toward the lighted lamp. He was sleeping in the same position he'd had inside his mother's belly, cheeks round, damp commas of hair on his forehead.

"What's his name?" I asked softly.

"Vincenzo," Adriana answered from the window.

I knelt beside the bed, I sniffed my nephew. He smelled clean, his head of still warm bread. I risked a caress, barely touching him.

"You'll have to keep us here for a little while," Adriana said. Her serious tone frightened me more than the request.

"I'll ask Piero."

"Piero is good, he'll want us for sure. Maybe you don't want us," and she turned again to look out, at the cones of white light from the street lamps on the pavement.

I left her there and went to the kitchen to boil some water. She rebelled at the cup of hot chamomile, but then blew over it to cool it and took it like a bitter syrup, in noisy sips followed by a grimace of disgust.

A brief moan from the baby, he uncurled his hands reflexively, but didn't wake up.

"Are you in danger?" I asked.

"Here, no," she said thoughtfully.

Afterward she went to the bathroom, still with one foot bare, one stuck in the sandal. I went over to Vincenzo, searching for similarities, but it was hard while he was sleeping, only his slightly impudent mouth seemed his mother's. And the shape of his nose recalled the other Vincenzo, the uncle he would never know.

In time he came increasingly to resemble him, in his face, in his way of walking, of laughing with his head thrown back. When his mother brought him to the town, people in the square stopped to look at him, so like the one who was no longer there. He also has the same determination, but my nephew knows where to apply it. At six he would concentrate for hours on his Lego bricks: he constructed ships complete in every detail. Now he wants to become a nautical engineer.

"I'll give you a thrashing if you don't study," his mother threatens him sometimes, but there's no need.

Adriana has been able to bring up a child different from our brother, different from her as well.

The child's name impressed me that night. Repeating it to myself later, I found it more right each time. Vincenzo sounds fresh and old in the same three syllables. Adriana has bound her child to a story of misfortunes and miracles, deaths and survivals: the unadorned story of our family. This Vincenzo seems to me stronger than the adversities, even now I would bet on his future.

3.

Yesterday I was called to the office in the late morning, during class. It was almost the end of the hour, we were talking about Francesco Biamonti. *Le parole la notte* is one of the novels I chose for this semester; it's not easy for my students, but they've become quite passionate about it. I wanted to challenge their understanding of Italian and some certainties about their own country.

Alain was struck by the "restless silences" of the protagonist and by the landscape, the Maritime Alps, which animate the story from the first page to the last. "Like punctuation," he said.

"You really feel as if you're in Liguria," the brown-haired girl who sits in the second row added.

"It's right there, after all, just beyond the border, a little farther south," and I pointed to the window.

Luc was moving around in his seat, preparing to speak. He wanted to read a sentence that insulted his national pride: "Every so often someone picks up France in his arms, displays it to the world, wanting us to believe that it's alive, but it's dead."

I anticipated him: "Should a critical gaze always be rejected or can it be useful for understanding what we can't see about ourselves?"

In the office a call from Italy was waiting for me, urgent. They had tried my cell phone, but it was switched off, the secretary said, covering the receiver. In the instant before answering I imagined the possible accidents, not that. Not this, which is keeping me awake in Room 405. Next door someone is returning, I hear the door and then peeing in the bathroom on the other side of the wall.

I didn't recognize the voice on the phone, and the dialect of Pescara sounded so unreal to me, at first.

"You got to get here, right away," and the rest was an agitated, confused mumble.

The phone call was brief, I said I would leave the next morning if I could get a seat on the train. When I hung up I couldn't breathe, I accepted the chair the secretary offered me. I remembered the breathing exercises that Piero had taught me the first time we went to Gran Sasso together. We climbed up the Direttissima route, on a day so clear that the mountain was a blinding basilica before our eyes. In one exposed place I had looked at the void below: it was a death so easy to take, you had merely to let go with your hands. Incapable of going on, I trembled, clutching the wall.

Sitting in the office at the University of Grenoble I practiced breathing with my diaphragm, regaining control. Someone offered me some water and I drank it. An entire past has called me back, like a coiled spring that suddenly lets go and returns to where it started.

Now I'm here. From outside, near the harbor, comes a mechanical hiss, amplified in the dark. It breaks off at regular intervals and so the silence becomes heavier. I don't know if Adriana hears the hiss, and the silence. Tomorrow I'll see her. Tomorrow is already today, 01:01 my wrist signals, phosphorescent, the double hour.

She didn't go back to sleep, either, the night she showed up at my house. In the morning she was waiting for me in the bathroom, sitting on the edge of the tub, with a towel over her shoulders and her hair washed.

"Come on, I don't want Piero to see me like this," she said, handing me the scissors.

I protested that I couldn't do it, she ought to go to the hairdresser.

"No, I'm embarrassed. It's not difficult, cut it short like this," and she touched above her ear.

She combed it very smooth, to make it easier for me. I began, the unsuitable scissors in one hand, locks of hair one by one in the fingers of the other. They fell with a dull thud on her legs, on the bottom of the tub, on the floor. Adriana had calmed down, I no longer felt her muscles contracted, her jaws locked.

"Where are you coming from?" I ventured.

"From a place you don't know," and she wiped some hair off the tip of her nose. "Now don't upset me with questions, cut and be quiet." She yawned with a cracking of bones. "You'll have to lend me something to put on, I came in a hurry," and she laughed for a second pulling up the edge of her nightgown.

"And for Vincenzo?" I asked her.

"He doesn't need milk, he still drinks mine. For the most urgent things you can go out later and get them."

"Me?"

"You. It's better if I stay inside for a while," and she closed her mouth in a way that admitted no response.

At the end she dried off, and dismay at the result gripped us: the hair was as if it had been bitten off, and she looked like a sick person, with her deep livid eye sockets. She wasn't angry; she asked me for Piero's electric razor and ran it over her head slowly, supporting the work of her hand with the movements of her neck.

"There, we'll start again from zero," she said, looking at herself in the mirror, almost pleased.

Suddenly she seemed so girlish, vulnerable as an egg. She was twenty-seven, but she made me want to protect her, to touch her bristling, perfect head, compared with the wild face. I grazed it for a moment with the tips of my fingers and she didn't pull back, so I spread my palm as if to contain her in a motionless caress, after all that time.

Then we went to the bedroom, to see Vincenzo. Adriana had put two pillows on the edge of the bed, so he wouldn't fall off. On the other side Piero was sleeping in his clothes on top of the sheets, turned toward the baby, one arm on the small body, but as gently as possible. From the window came the first light of day, still gray, and the sounds of the city waking, the garbage trucks out picking up trash. Adriana let an exclamation of surprise escape and, without moving, Piero opened his eyes.

"This I really wasn't expecting from you," he said to her with a nod toward the baby.

He had returned silently and heard our voices in the bathroom. It took a moment to understand and then he lay down next to the new thing, stretching out, down to his tanned feet.

In the kitchen he joked with Adriana about her new hairdo and stopped me, touching my wrist, while I was lighting the stove for the coffee. Close up he had a faint hospital smell, he'd come home with disinfectants and suffering tangled up on him. I asked how his father was, he reassured me.

"Set the table in the dining room, it's a morning to celebrate," he said, going out. His mother had got him used to that and so for the occasion I did it: linen tablecloth, china cups, silver spoons from among our wedding presents. I arranged them, lost in thought, for Adriana whom I heard moving in the other room, for her baby who had been in my life for a few hours. A future completely different from what I imagined had just arrived.

"Here's your aunt," she introduced me when Vincenzo woke up.

She wanted to give him to me, but he formed his lips into a

cry and I drew back. He looked around with dark, mobile eyes. He wrinkled his forehead in a grimace and immediately smoothed it, reassured by the contact with his mother. Curious, he touched her shaved head. Adriana changed him, she had some diapers in her bag, then she unbuttoned her nightgown and offered him her breast, sitting on my bed. Vincenzo drank till he was full, every so often moving his hand on her blue-veined breast. I couldn't believe that my sister, so thin, was capable of all that milk: a rivulet ran from the corner of his mouth to his neck. With his oblique gaze he made sure that I remained at a safe distance. He was already nine months old.

Piero returned with wild flowers found at a neighborhood market and *cornetti* from the *pasticceria* Renzi, still warm. Adriana grabbed one immediately and ate half in a single bite.

"That's a table for rich people," she commented, arranging the bouquet in a vase.

The child let his uncle hold him and smiled as if in their brief sleep together they had become intimate. I brought the coffeepot from the kitchen, with the last drops still sputtering. We sat down, Vincenzo in Piero's arms, Adriana next to him. She gave the tail of the *cornetto* to her son. We were like a family enjoying our breakfast time.

Suddenly there was a knock at the door, repeated several times. Adriana jumped up, bumping a leg of the table, and the coffeepot tipped. I caught it, but I burned my hand. She ran into the bathroom, forgetting even Vincenzo.

A dish towel belonging to the woman upstairs had fallen onto our balcony. She didn't know we had a nephew, what a nice child, and the mamma was there, yes, only she'd gone in the other room for a moment. Now we, too, would want to have one, she said, and took one of his hands and waved it cheerfully. For Vincenzo it was too much, his mother who had disappeared without warning, the unknown woman who talked to him and touched him: he began to cry, at first softly and then with all the power of his little voice. Not even that served to flush Adriana out of her hiding place, or maybe she couldn't hear him, huddled in a corner the way she used to sometimes in our house in the town, with her hands pressed to her ears. I called her and she didn't answer. I moved the bathroom door handle up and down, I banged on the door with my fists. The neighbor didn't interest me at all. It was always like that with my sister, at any moment she can arouse in me overwhelming tenderness or furious rage.

"Adriana, come out and take your son," I shouted.

I waited for a reaction that didn't come.

I went back and gave the speechless woman her dish towel. I hastily said goodbye to her. Meanwhile Piero tried to calm Vincenzo, showing him something in the attempt to distract him: the waves so close through the window open to the sea, a boat moving, but the child's gaze didn't go that far. All he wanted was his mother. As soon as I closed the front door, Adriana came out with a fresh face, picked up her son, who held out his arms to her, and the crying stopped as if she had touched a secret switch.

"You think you're good, but inside you're mean," she didn't fail to say to me before sitting down again at the table to finish breakfast.

Piero and I had collapsed together on the couch, I could feel the sweat evaporating from his skin. We weren't used to the confusion brought by children. Some couples among our friends had them, little ones: from a distance we liked other people's. Our children were still a vague plan, not a true desire; a fantasy, rather, necessary but not sufficient.

After a few minutes I got up, I had to settle the two of them in the room and go out, get what Vincenzo needed. Piero stretched out his legs and fell asleep, recovering from the night in the hospital with his father and the morning's surprises.

That night we talked about it. I was already in bed when he

came home; he turned on the bedside lamp and leaned over to kiss the back of my neck, on my preferred vertebra. The light rustling of the shirt laid on the chair, the shoes taken off near the window.

"My girl is awake," he whispered, bringing to the sheets the mint of his breath and a residue of cheer from the meeting he had just left.

"You have to excuse Adriana," I said. "She showed up without warning, but I don't think she and the baby will stay long."

He turned out the light and hugged me from behind, he liked to sleep that way.

"I'm glad to see them around the house. Vincenzo is adorable, and your sister always makes me laugh."

"Me not so much," I said, taking his hand.

He rubbed the tip of his nose against my shoulder as if to scratch an itch. Then he muffled a cry against my back, but joking: "You have cold feet even in summer."

"And yours are scalding."

"Now I'll warm yours," he said in a sleepy voice.

I felt his body lose all its tension, let go around me. His hand relaxed in mine. I would stay like that until morning, awake in a safe place.

4.

I didn't think I'd find my students still there when I returned to get my bag with the books. Nor did I want to see them, at that moment. But the dark-haired girl in the second row had waited for me. Her name is Béatrice, but I've heard her insist on the Italian pronunciation of her name. When I entered the classroom, she picked up a notebook on the desk and came toward me with her backpack. I gathered up the scattered papers, piled them trembling on top of one another, paying no attention to the order or the side of the page. Out of the corner of my eye I registered her movement in my direction, annoyed by that insistence when the class time was up.

"Excuse me, I had another question," she said, but her voice betrayed an exaggerated apprehension.

"Can't we talk about it next week? I have to go now." And I closed the zipper on my bag brusquely.

Then I made the mistake of pausing for a moment, and I recognized in her something of myself. I couldn't leave her so mortified and disappointed. She seemed about to cry and I couldn't bear it, not yesterday. I made an effort to be kind.

"I'm listening."

"I think the protagonist of the novel is Veronique. She has all the others circling around her, especially the men. But what is her power, besides beauty?"

"Maybe the loss she carries inside," I answered, looking straight at her.

She gave the impression of having just got out of bed, on her eyelids was the smudged liner of the day before.

"Where is your family from?" I asked her, out of politeness.

"My grandparents are Sicilian, but when they came to Grenoble they made my father speak French only. For them Italian was the language of shame, because of the Fascist occupation here."

She doesn't know it, but our emigrants were ashamed mainly of being poor. Certainly Béatrice will get the highest mark on the exam. In the little time she managed to get from me she summarized the story of her family—that's what she wants to make peace with. I encouraged her: she'll discover later, on her own, how difficult it is to find peace. For twenty minutes she was able to suspend the effect of the news I had received.

I returned from the campus on the tram, looking out. In the weak sunlight some students were working in the small gardens assigned to them. Others were swarming toward the cafeteria, they were organizing a demonstration against reform of the university. A wild rabbit crossed the lawn, stopping every two or three hops, as if unsure of his direction.

I continued the day according to the set schedule, only I forgot to have lunch. No stimulus arrived from an empty stomach. I kept walking out of habit, passing the entrance to the house and the pet food store. At a certain point I no longer knew where I was. The good thing about Grenoble is that you just have to look toward the end of the street: "*Au bout de chaque rue, une montagne* /A mountain at the end of every street," Stendhal wrote. Chartreuse, Belledonne, and Vercors are majestic reference points, casting their shadows over the city. Piero would have loved them, if he had come to see me. He said more than once, when I returned to Pescara on vacation or he telephoned me to say happy birthday: "As soon as I'm free, I'll go climbing in your area."

Adriana is the one who actually came, no one else in the

family. I had gotten the job a few months earlier and was shar-
ing an attic apartment with a colleague in the history department. Adriana had asked for my address to send me a postcard. She appeared on a rainy night with Vincenzo, who was
five and crying with weariness. They had changed trains in
Bologna and Turin, then in Chambéry, I still can't figure out
how they didn't get lost. Until that moment she had traveled
only by hitchhiking, in her wilder years.

"I came to see if you're comfortable here," she said, offering me *bocconotti* cookies, carefully wrapped.

I can picture my nephew in the cable car, the next day. He
wanted to go up and down a hundred times, his hands opened
against the plexiglass, his lips an O of perfect surprise. Adriana
admired the three towers built by Italian masons in the sixties,
she compared them with the tallest buildings in Pescara.

I still go up to the Bastille every so often on a Sunday in
good weather, but I walk. Like a lot of people, my friend Théa
and I enjoy the physical exercise. We mingle with the tourists
who are afraid to go in the cable car or feel the need to get
there the hard way. The younger ones who are in shape run in
shorts and running shoes on the unpaved road that winds up
to the fortress. I hear the labored breath as their lean bodies
pass us.

It's the panorama from above that I'm looking for, a clearer
air. I see the old city, where I live, so dense and recognizable
from up there, a hot dark core surrounded by the concrete that
came later. Later we meet other friends at the Café de la Table
Ronde. Sitting outside, we drink Martini *bianco*, time flows
alcoholic and light.

I've taken off the watch and am lost in the length of this
night. No voices or steps can be heard in the street, or the
clang of the manhole cover under the tires of the cars. My
phone vibrates, a message asks if I'm awake, if we can meet

tomorrow morning at eight in front of the hotel. From the room upstairs come the moans of sex, but it doesn't last long, they must be tired. My memory, on the other hand, isn't tired, it stirs up random recollections, seething out of control.

I had an appointment with Yvette yesterday afternoon, and I went. Her shop is in Rue de Bonne, a few blocks from home. She's an exaggerated, middle-aged blonde, with lipstick that fades into the wrinkles crowding her lips. She's not exactly a gossip, but her chat induces clients to confidences. She is the depot for all the stories of the neighborhood, and even I talk a little, but only about my French life. I tell her about the cat Hector, who is half mine and half my neighbor's. She's amused by this domestic animal that goes between the two apartments and eats on the landing, where we also keep the plants. Yvette pretends to forget the answer from last time and keeps asking me if Christophe and I are going out. Meanwhile she proposes some highlights, a more informal cut. Maybe she hopes that something romantic will occur.

She saw me come in yesterday with an altered look. There were only two clients, already in the hands of the assistants. She insisted on washing my hair herself, and went ahead of me into the back of the salon, holding aside the black curtain. I sat in the first chair, they were all empty, settled my neck in the hollow and then down, with my head back.

Yvette adjusted the water temperature. She diluted the shampoo in a bowl and poured it on with a certain gravity, as if for a baptism. She began massaging my scalp with circular movements of her fingertips, and the shampoo foamed, rustling. She asked me if something had happened.

"I have to go back to Italy."

When she got near the temples the tears were released. They dripped from my eyes to my ears, my soapy hair, Yvette's hands. She stopped, she held my head, in silence. We waited for the moment to pass.

Afterward she dried my hair, rotating the brush; in the mirror her fingers moved rapidly like the legs of a spider. One client said goodbye and left, proud of her new hair style, one was commenting on the latest episode of *Julie Lescaut* with the girl who was shaping her curls. Yvette asked me where in Italy I was from. She had never heard of Abruzzo: it's even with Rome, I told her, on the sea on the other side.

"I dream of the sea," she sighed.

In the end she mussed my hair a little, blowing warm air from the dryer, for a more natural effect. She shaped some parts with gel.

"So we'll see you when you get back," and she took off the robe.

I stopped in front of the display windows on the other side of the street, as if I were returning for summer vacation or Christmas, as if nothing had happened. I never arrived without presents for Vincenzo: I chose two T-shirts with Astérix on the chest and some butter cookies. He still likes to nibble them on the couch, in front of the cartoons. Now he watches *Family Guy*.

Adriana had brought so little the night she took refuge with me in Via Zara, with the baby and a bag. She'd grabbed some diapers, a pacifier, and a soft elephant in the rush to escape. I began then to buy him food and clothes.

That first day I left them in the house, sister and nephew, and went out with Piero. As soon as we were outside the wind hit us, rising to drive out the muggy air that had stagnated over the city for days. The sand flew everywhere, from the beach nearby. A short stretch together, as far as his office, and we separated.

"Don't worry about spending for the baby," he said, resting his index finger on my nose.

We kissed goodbye and I turned to watch him as he opened the entrance door. Muscles trained by climbing were a landscape tense under the blue shirt.

Some Sundays I went with him, and in front of the wall I witnessed the hand to hand between him and the rock. I admired the grace; the leaps from one outcrop to the next left me breathless. The stubborn work of arms and legs, hands and feet, of all his fingers tired my neck, my eyes. He got smaller and smaller, a stain of color high up, attached to the rock and to life. When he descended he still belonged to the mountain, to the light he had seen up there. His companions cheered him, among them some who had recently joined the group. With me he was affectionate but distant, and then I was jealous of the Apennines.

I returned from shopping tired of the wind, grains of sand squeaky between my teeth. The door of the guest room was ajar, I heard Vincenzo's babbling, my sister talking sweetly to him. She was sitting on the bed, next to him, but when I came in the air made the shutters bang and she jumped up with a cry.

"Are you crazy?" she asked, one hand to her chest.

"Even the wind scares you? Who's after you, the devil?"

"Well, just about," escaped her.

She sat down next to the baby again, looked up at me from below with her mouth shut; it couldn't say. I pulled out of the bags the clothes I'd bought for Vincenzo, and she was excited for a moment by a tiny pair of jeans, with adjustable elastic. There was also a flowered dress for her, with straps. Adriana has always had a weakness for summer dresses, she would have liked a hundred every season. Even the ones from the street market were fine, ankle-length or above the knee. I held the dress in front of her and she admired it for a long time, feeling between thumb and index finger the lightness of the fabric. Afterward her eyes were damp, shining with a desperation. She swallowed to keep from crying.

"You're nuts, you wasted a pile of money," and she shook her head.

She asked if I'd gotten pastina for Vincenzo, it was almost

time for his lunch. We went to the other room to prepare it, she with her son astride her bony hip.

"Who are you afraid of?" I asked.

I waited, but the little stars cooked in silence and the sound of the sea outside. I put oil and parmigiano on them, she sat at the table with Vincenzo on her lap and began feeding him. She was repeating the gestures I'd seen at the house in the town when she was still a child and, at nearly every meal, used to feed our brother Giuseppe.

"Did you steal something?" I provoked her.

She stopped the back and forth of the spoon between bowl and mouth.

"Where's that coming from?"

"It wouldn't be the first time," I let slip.

She stirred the pastina and went back to Vincenzo.

"No one likes to steal. What do you know about it, you're not in need of anything."

We both understood what I was talking about. That winter she had lost her job, but something would turn up, as usual, according to her there was never anything to worry about. Or she would return to the town for a while, to our parents' house. I had offered her some money, but she twisted her mouth. It was Piero's and my first year as a married couple.

"If I need money I'll get it from you," she had assured me, with that distracted air.

Outside it had been trying to snow for a while, we had moved closer to the balcony and each other. The flakes fell obliquely, the beach slowly whitened, rippled like a desert of sugar. Our breath condensed into steam on the glass, along with some mute thoughts.

"Will you lend me that really long scarf with all the colors?" Adriana asked.

"I'll find it for you," and I went into the bedroom.

She waited for me there, with her gaze on the gray waves.

Suddenly she was in a hurry, she had remembered an interview for a job. She wound the wool around her neck many times and kissed me hard on one cheek.

The next morning two men came to hang curtains at the windows. I couldn't pay them. The snow had disappeared, like the money from the purse lying on a table. I waited a few days before going to see her, I was afraid to confront her. She denied having taken the money, and was offended by my suspicions.

"Your students cheated you and you didn't even notice," she said without losing her composure.

We quarreled bitterly, but also like children, pushing and shoving. Adriana knew how to bring me back, to all that I had wanted to leave. I had been working for a short time with Morelli at the University of Chieti, I wouldn't let her hold me down. Parents and brothers, the town in the hills, were far away, in the harshness of dialect. They occupied memories that were not happy, and barely encroached on the present. She, on the contrary, was always so alive and dangerous. I felt intensely the unease of being her sister.

5.

I wake up suddenly from a short deep sleep. I want to move my arm and it doesn't respond. For a few moments I don't know where I am, there's nothing familiar in the darkness, Hector's purring in the background as he curls around my feet is missing. I felt pain, yesterday, and I don't remember the origin. I feel it now, too, it's that weight on my chest, but I don't recognize it. I grope for the light switch, in the lamplight the strange hotel room brings back the truth.

I put my jacket on over my shoulders and go out to the balcony, shivering, under this sky of migrating clouds. Across the road the Adriatic is only a shade of black, which bathes the sand and retreats. I can't see the sea but I've always known it's there. The fishermen of Borgo Sud must be at sea, as usual, already at work. Everyone else is sleeping, it's too late for the day that's over, too early for the new one. Adriana is also sleeping, a bit of the sea has dripped into her name.

The three years of difference have become invisible, but when we were younger they counted. That's what I thought, Adriana never agreed. Sometimes I wanted to take charge, as the older sister.

"You have a head just for books," she said.

It was the voice of her admiration, and also a way of putting me down.

So I decided to take her to the town with Vincenzo, our parents must have known of that turn in her life. We were making dinner and she wouldn't stop listing the wrongs she had suffered as a girl. They had taken her out of school at fifteen, sent her to work in the countryside: grape harvest, olive harvest. No one in the family thought she ought to continue school beyond the middle school diploma she had narrowly earned. Our brothers mocked her ambition to become a surveyor, our mother was silent.

Together we fought all summer, finally in September our father gave a reluctant assent: Adriana could enroll in a technical institute in Pescara, share a room with me at Signora Bice's. After the enthusiasm of the early days the long afternoons in our few square meters were difficult for her, she measured them from one side to the other with the steps of a tiger in captivity. Sometimes she opened a book, and, flopped on the bed, she'd read half a page as if it were written in a foreign language. I didn't understand that her inability to concentrate was obedience: Adriana was making our father's prediction come true.

"You'll be back to eat the favas, you won't make it to the end of the year," he had said when she came home with the report card from the first semester.

For a few days in April she reappeared at Signora Bice's with the innocent hunger of someone coming home from school, but her face was red. After lunch she sat at the desk and meticulously forged the signature in the attendance book. If I came near she covered it with a notebook. We were no longer children, mutual secrets had grown up with us.

Our father came to get her one Thursday, he didn't wait for us to return to the town on the Saturday bus. Certainly Signora Bice had called him, suspicious of Adriana's early tan. He had stationed himself at the end of the school day on the street where the school was, but she didn't come from there. She came from the direction of the sea, with the slightly hesitant gait of someone who has been in the sun too long. She had spent the whole morning with a young fisherman; they had also been on his boat at the port, but this Adriana told me only much later. I imagine her still dreamy eyes when our father appeared before her.

"The way they treated us, it would have been better if they hadn't had children," she said, furiously slicing tomatoes in the kitchen at my house.

She didn't mention all her absences and I didn't remind her of them. They could never justify the behavior of our parents.

"You can forget about my coming," my sister concluded as we were sitting at the table.

But she changed her mind at the most inconvenient moment. I was packing a small suitcase for two days in Rome with Piero. I liked going to conferences with him in the cities where there was art: for us they were still brief honeymoons.

"Tomorrow is fine," Adriana said passing my room.

She had already subverted our habits, as she always does with whoever is around her.

"Go, before she has second thoughts," Piero advised me.

The next morning we were all leaving early. At the last minute he gave me his paper to read, a passage seemed to him a little confused. We leaned over the table to correct it, I simplified it, taking out the repetitious parts.

"I'd be lost without my professor," he joked.

In the doorway Adriana, with her son in her arms and the purse over her shoulder, was trembling, the current of her impatience reached us.

"Please, don't get mad at her," Piero said, picking up his pages.

With a cramp of longing I saw him leave.

We were no longer the girls who followed the road home from the height of the bus. The weeds on the side of the road were so close Adriana could touch them with her palm that cut the air outside the window. She hadn't been that way for a long time, everything seemed to her different and curious.

At the curve where the dredge was she signaled me to pull over. The place was no longer as she remembered it. There were no cows, the barbed wire of the enclosure had rusted out here and there. The windows of the farmhouse were all shut and no farmers were at work around it.

We saw a big field of sunflowers, facing toward the horizon where dawn appeared every day. In the same direction our brother, many years before, had flown off the skidding motorcycle to land with his most vulnerable part, his neck, on the iron spikes.

"All these flowers are for your uncle Vincenzo," Adriana said to her son, as soon as she got out of the car.

She raised him up to the corollas, which were taller than us, and he touched one. We stayed there a few moments, gripped by the sight. Certainly whoever planted them hadn't been sitting on his tractor thinking of the boy who had died there in a long-ago autumn, but truly the sunflowers seemed dedicated to him.

As soon as I started the car, my sister sketched three signs of the cross on her forehead, mouth, and chest, ending with a kiss on her index finger, which she tossed out the window. Then in silence we followed a truck to the town, not finding along the curves a space to pass it.

"They're downstairs," Adriana guessed, smelling a familiar odor when we arrived in front of the building.

They had opened the garage. Our father was standing outside, turning peppers on the grill with his bare hands, holding them by the stem. On the ground was a basket half full of raw ones, on an oval plate set on an overturned box were some already roasted. He used his left hand as tongs, since he had lost his index and middle fingers in his last stint working at the kiln.

She was sitting right inside, facing the morning light, holding on her legs a wooden board where she was stripping the peppers of skin and seeds. She saw us right away, as we were coming from the square, Adriana behind me carrying the child. Our mother paused a moment with the knife in midair, then she lowered her head and began scraping in a greater hurry.

When I greeted them she was silent; she must be mad at me, since now I phoned and that was all, skipping the usual weekly visit.

"So you weren't dead," our father said, not looking at Adriana, not responding to her hello. Then he continued his activity with basket, coal, plate.

Vincenzo called attention to himself with one of his babblings, reaching out toward all those new things. His grandfather, unaware, looked at him sideways, without sympathy.

"Now you're bringing the kids you take care of?" he asked his daughter.

"Are you blind? You don't see he's the image of her, you don't see he's hers?" our mother shouted at him, throwing board and knife on the concrete floor.

Jumping to her feet she ran her dirty hands over her face, from the forehead down. I went over to calm her and she pushed me away, but then she grabbed me and shook me by the shoulder.

"I trusted you and instead you bit your tongue and didn't tell us anything," she shouted at me.

I felt on my skin the drops of saliva, the rage she shifted onto me to spare Adriana, protected by the child she held in her arms. So small, he was sacred even there.

Someone looked out the window, a neighbor asked from above what was happening. My mother loosened her grip, then left me. She moved to go back up to the house, but after a few meters she stopped to catch her breath, one hand pressed to her hip. Then Adriana said between her teeth: "It's not her fault, she didn't know."

Vincenzo began to cry.

"Now what am I supposed to do? Can I feed him upstairs or do we have to go?" she asked our father. She hid the effort to keep her voice firm, not to give in herself to tears or shouts.

"Where would you take him, to the café?" he said. He started off ahead of us: like the head of the family furious but respectful of an ancient hospitality he led the way to the second floor.

They left us with the baby and went back down to finish the job. Adriana changed him and I made the pastina, then she put him to sleep in his grandparents' room, leaving it open so she would hear him if he woke up. The room that as girls we shared with our brothers was closed, she went in. Our bunk bed was gone, a woolen quilt covered Sergio's bed: the last night he'd spent there before leaving for Libya was in winter. There was no trace of the others, Domenico lived in the country-side and Giuseppe in an institution where he was taken care of. Without them the house was cleaner, orderly, the parents alone. They still packed in supplies for a large family they no longer had.

With automatic gestures Adriana brought in the dry clothes from the line on the balcony and began to fold them, piling them on a chair. She moved aside when our mother returned, loaded with bags full of peppers to freeze. She had left some on a platter for lunch, and a tied-up bag that I would find later in my purse, for Piero, who loved them. She spread the checked tablecloth on the table and put out four plates. She ordered me to finish setting the table, indicating the drawer with the silverware. Out of the corner of my eye I saw her go back and forth between the two bedrooms, she was bringing other pillows to make a barrier around Vincenzo's sleep. Then she returned to the kitchen, in a moment she'd seasoned the peppers: oil and salt, chopped garlic and parsley.

"Take off that hat and cut the bread," she said without turning to Adriana.

My sister obeyed; her hair, which had grown a few millimeters, was ignored. We sat at the table, one on each side, silent,
only the noise of chairs shifted. We were sweating even without moving.

"There's no wine or did you forget it?" our father asked at
a certain point.

I got up, there was the remains of a bottle behind the curtain under the sink. I poured the red into a glass and then there
was none left. He drank it and smacked his tongue, looking at
Adriana at the other end of the table, who was mopping up the
flavored oil with a piece of bread.

"What did you name your son?"

"Vincenzo."

Our mother brought her hand to her mouth and got up.
She took some steps toward her bedroom, but she must have
remembered that the baby was there. She shut herself in the
children's room.

"You've already lost the father?" he resumed in the silence
that followed.

From the square rose voices, a loud laugh. Without taking
his eyes off Adriana, who didn't answer, he pushed his empty
plate away.

"And how will you provide for him?" he insisted.

She sat up, placed on a blue square of the tablecloth the
crust she was holding in her fingers.

"Better than you did for me, you want to bet?"

We left as soon as the baby woke up. We were on our way
when I saw our mother in the rearview mirror. If I hadn't
offered her a ride she would have gone on foot as always, two
kilometers there and two back, or someone from the town
might have given her a lift. In front of the cemetery she left us
without a word. It was the last time Adriana saw her. My sister's prodigious intuition didn't help her, she didn't know how
to recognize any warning sign in the bent figure walking along

the gravel path between the cypresses. So they didn't set aside the bitterness and didn't say goodbye, they didn't give each other a conciliatory hug.

Adriana was too far from death to have a presentiment of it and, like all young people, she trusted in the eternity of parents.

6.

The next day I had to take her in the car "to a place." We were skirting the right bank of the river when she asked me to stop. We continued on foot, Adriana always a little ahead, straight and concentrated on the road. Small salty waves went upstream from the mouth, confusing my view.

"Couldn't we go later, when it's cooler?" I asked.

"Some things have to be done in the heat of the day," my sister answered, turning toward Borgo Sud.

Certainly she, too, was suffering in the straw hat pushed down on her head and the sunglasses she hadn't asked to borrow. We went in among the low working-class apartment buildings and one- and two-story houses. I had never been in that neighborhood, but I knew that Adriana had been hanging around there for years.

The city surprised me, revealed itself as larger, different from my imaginary map, which was limited to the center and a few areas on the outskirts. Some walls were painted with naïve motifs, I lingered a moment to look at one depicting a muscular sailor pulling his boat onshore, in the background sails in the wind.

No one passed on the street, on foot or in a car, the shutters were closed, the fish delivery vans drawn up on the sidewalks. It seemed a separate place, where time ran more slowly and other rules were in force. An invisible border isolated it from Pescara all around. But it was clean, not even a scrap of paper tossed on the ground.

Adriana realized that I was behind and she turned back to pull me by the arm.

"It's not a tour, hurry up," she said between her teeth. "After lunch the people who aren't on the sea sleep," she added, lowering her voice as if we could wake them.

But a bare-chested man was eating watermelon on a shaded first-floor balcony. He stopped with the piece in midair when he saw us. He spit out some seeds. Under that gaze Adriana moved haltingly, a sign that she was afraid. At a certain point she turned back suddenly, I followed her into the shelter of a building. Shouts could be heard behind us, they might be the man's.

We walked for a while at a quick pace, but as if to no purpose. Finally, after looking around several times, she led me to the back of a green house. We stood listening to all that silence, then she stuck her arm between the bars of a small gate and found by touch the key to open it, as if it were a habitual gesture.

"What are you doing, where are we going?" I protested in a whisper.

"I told you, I have to get some stuff, it'll just take a second."

She pulled me inside something that wasn't a courtyard or a porch or a yard, but showed traces of recent family life. On one side some plants struggled in the dry earth, next to a folded chaise and a closed umbrella. The rest of the space was protected by a corrugated lean-to roof: it covered a platform with a gas stove and a sink, a table with a plastic tablecloth and unmatching chairs around it. In one corner yellow fishing boots and knotted nets, perhaps to be repaired. The sirocco of the past days had spread a coating of sand everywhere. The French doors were open and the glass broken, the shards squeaked under Adriana's footsteps.

"You wait here and if you hear something strange, whistle," she said on the threshold.

She didn't give me time to remind her that I didn't know
how to whistle. She crossed one room and another, then I
heard her go up the stairs. She moved warily, ears pricked to
the slightest noise, but also with the confidence of someone
who had lived in that house. I didn't want to stay outside without her. I went into the half light of a kitchen, except that on
one side was a single bed, at its feet the cradle where Vincenzo
had slept. I recognized from the tangled sheets my sister who
had waked suddenly and thrown them off.

The furnishings were simple but careful in every detail. A
shelf held a collection of shells, arranged from the smallest to
the largest, with the golden whorls displayed. Leaning against
the television some books: *A Hundred Fish Recipes, The Sea Is
Served* the spines said.

I recognized Adriana's hand everywhere, but the impression of my alienation from what she had achieved there chilled
me.

Next to the door through which we had entered a water-
proof sailor's jacket hung on a hook. A strong smell of rot saturated the place, and I looked around: in the sink there was a
plate turned upside down on another. I lifted it, freeing a fly
that rose into the air. Slices of raw meat were swarming with
white larvae, small slow lucky worms on all that food that had
been left there to thaw. I saw the date on a calendar with
detachable pages hanging on the wall: ten days had passed
since Adriana's flight.

I stepped on something soft on the tile floor: the lock of
hair that was missing when she arrived at my house. On the
table a glass held a note written in the labored handwriting of
someone who rarely uses a pen: "If you come back ring my bell
I'll help you."

It was signed Isolina.

Adriana came down the stairs like a hurricane.

"Let's go," she said.

She gave me some bags she'd filled, supermarket bags, she carried a bulging tote. I'd put the two plates in a bag to throw them away with their contents. She returned the gate key to its place and we left, then we had to get through the neighborhood again. We set off, quickly but without running, constantly looking behind. Malicious eyes were pointed at us from the upper floors, or maybe I only imagined them. I shared Adriana's fear without knowing what risk I was running. In the preceding days I hadn't managed to get a word out of her about what had happened. Sometimes her confidences were a long time coming, even now.

I told her breathlessly about the message on the table.

"Oh, how sweet Isolina is," she said abruptly. "She lives next door."

Suddenly a weedy field opened up amid the buildings. Children were playing in shorts, their T-shirts were stains of color on the sunburned grass. Some were busy behind a row of corrugated metal sheds, around something, or someone.

"It's Lelé—who knows what they're doing to him," Adriana murmured between her teeth, slowing down. She was undecided for a moment, then she kept going straight. We were already breathing the dense humidity of the river when she stopped suddenly, seized by a thought.

"I forgot something important, I have to go get it. You take this stuff to the car and move it down by the waterfront, I'll be there in a quarter of an hour," and she immediately retraced her steps. She turned a moment for an instruction, a cry in the air: "If you don't see me go home and look after the baby."

I waited for her where she had told me, counting the minutes. I got out of the car, inside it was unbearable. Outside there was no longer any breeze, not a shadow nearby to shelter me. The air was salty and tasted intensely of the sea: it dried out your mouth. A woman crossed the street, carrying a straw purse with her rolled-up beach mat sticking out of it. She looked at me as if my presence among the waves of heat that trembled on the asphalt were inexplicable to her.

Adriana's quarter of an hour extended, it never expired. It ended suddenly and time began to flow. I saw her dead, killed by a knife in the chest, a chokehold on her neck, or randomly run over by someone, with that habit she had of rushing into the street without looking. I've always been afraid for her, so rash and drifting. We lived together for a couple of years, when I was about to graduate, and studied after dinner sitting at the kitchen table, under the circle of fluorescent light. Adriana never came home. Around two or three in the morning I had collapsed with my head on the book, exhausted by waiting for the slightest sound: her key pushed into the lock, the proof that she had survived another night of forays into the city.

How long could I wait for her? In the inescapable light the portent of her last words seemed to me already truth: at home Piero was looking after the baby, certainly awake by now.

When she appeared beside the door, I didn't even know where she'd come from. She was holding something under her arm, wrapped in newspaper.

"Come on, how long does it take to get going?" She was annoyed immediately.

She took off the hat and placed it in back, carefully, on what she had gone to get. Drops of sweat sparkled on the few millimeters her hair had grown, like tiny diamonds.

We were silent until we got to the bridge over the river, in the angry traffic of the summer afternoon. Adriana had taken off my sandals and put her feet on the air-conditioning vent.

"I wonder if Vincenzo cried with Piero," I said softly.

"Your husband knows how to take care of babies," she answered thoughtfully.

"And Rafael? Is he the father?"

"When he was there he always had Vincenzo playing with him," she recalled, her voice cracking.

"And now where is he?" I asked.

She told me with her left hand not to insist, she was looking at the Upim department store to hide her emotion.

"What was there so important still, in the house?" I asked after a few minutes, waiting for a light.

"Now you'll see," and Adriana reached toward the back seat.

She tore off the paper around what seemed a picture, looking at it sideways. Big Vincenzo, as she now called him, was with his friend the Gypsy: they were smiling in black and white, both holding cigarettes. In the background, the merry-go-round moving in a blur, and then a field, under the cloudless sky. Another Gypsy had brought it to us, some months after the funeral, and Adriana had wanted it for herself. In the town she had it on the wall opposite her bed, we looked at it every morning as soon as we woke up.

In that house that was all hers she had gone to retrieve a piece of our memory.

7

Rafael was the one who took her out on the boat when my sister skipped school at fifteen. They'd go on board days when the Invincible was docked at the quay, swaying in the water at the mouth of the river. The first time they had sex on an old mattress amid piled up polystyrene chests and the smell of fish. Rafael would lie down there to sleep on cold nights at sea, after dropping the nets or the traps with bunches of laurel to attract the squid. He saw the red rivulet dripping. He collected it on his finger and licked it, curious. It must have been Adriana's blood that bound them for life, "like a love potion," she told me in a moment of adult intimacy.

At first Rafael was careful not to hurt her, but "later he was a bull," she explained, eyes flashing. "When he gets off the boat he has only one thing in mind," she added, and she didn't at all dislike it.

I also heard her boast about Rafael's desires with people she hardly knew. I listened in silence, it embarrassed me to talk about intimacy between Piero and me with a sister who didn't know shame. Sometimes she'd ask, with a mixture of worry and pity: "Do you and Piero enjoy life?"

Rafael immediately introduced her to friends as his girl-friend: *guagliona mi'*. He was nineteen when he met her. He had been fatherless since he was a child, and he worked on his uncle's Invincible with the fixed dream of buying a boat of his own. When they returned in the middle of the night to unload the fish and didn't even turn off the engines in the rush to go out again, his mother brought him a thermos of coffee and the *ciambellone* just out of the oven. She walked along the quay in the moonlight, a figure in slippers whom the sailors recognized from a distance, with her flowered bathrobe buttoned in front and during the cold months a shapeless coat over her shoulders. That mother was Isolina.

Rafael and Adriana didn't lose touch when my father pulled her out of school and brought her back to the town. As soon as possible she'd jump on a bus and join him, the days when there was no fishing. All she needed was to scrape together the change for the ticket and she left with no thought but the urgency of finding him. She returned to shouted reprimands and beatings, but she almost didn't feel them, in that weariness after love. For the first time she gave in to someone.

I no longer counted for her. She hid from me her trips to Pescara, maybe she didn't even remember that I was there, too.

"Your sister's gone crazy for someone, a Gypsy, I'm sure. Have you seen them together?" our mother asked when I came home on Saturdays. The improbability of meeting them in a city of a hundred thousand inhabitants escaped her.

In the autumn Adriana picked grapes, olives in the surrounding countryside or in the neighborhood of Ortona. Strawberries in spring. Some mornings she went out at six as usual, but didn't show up in the square for the bus that carried the sleepy women to work.

Then I really did run into them, at the feast of Sant'Andrea. I was staying with Giuditta on those burning-hot evenings of late July. We had just finished our graduation exam and wanted to make up for the nights spent translating Plutarch and Xenophon.

Like us, they were walking in the crowd that streamed from the beach after the fireworks display on the water. The echo of the bangs lingered in our ears, the smell of gunpowder stung in the air. He had an arm around her shoulders, his fingers dangling on her breast, a silver ring showing on his ring finger. She wore one that was identical, she'd take it off and put it aside whenever they fought, but didn't lose it.

They always loved each other, in that passionate and irregular way of theirs. They left each other out of a wish to find each other again. Then something else separated them, which Adriana called bad luck, envy, or the wickedness of certain people.

At the feast she heard her name shouted and she turned, sketching a flaming wheel with her ruffled orange dress. She had never been so beautiful nor was she later, not ever again.

The light went out of her face for a moment, when she saw me.

"This is my sister who goes to school," she said to him, and Rafael crushed my hand in his big rough palm. Each of his black curls vibrated with the strength of his grip.

He insisted on buying a gelato for me and Giuditta, and we headed toward the main street. People were lingering along the shore, carrying glasses out of the beach clubs, which were all still open and illuminated. Istria, Calypso, La Capponcina, we passed one after the other as we walked side by side along the sea.

Giuditta twisted her head to study Rafael's muscles, since he was next to her. Apart from the T-shirt and shorts he resembled Michelangelo's *David*, of which we knew even the protruding veins of arms and hands. Adriana noticed her clinging gaze and with a skip placed herself between them, blocking her view.

We were in a perfect tie in the usual dilemma for the inhabitants of Pescara: a cone from Berardo or Camplone? The inimitable whipped cream that one of them put on top won.

When the voice arrived behind her, Adriana was choosing her flavors with her eager finger on the glass of the counter.

"My treat," Vittorio said.

He, too, had come to the city for the fireworks of Sant'Andrea, and separated from his group as soon as he saw that so familiar and desired figure. What luck it must have seemed to him, to find her there by chance. They had grown up together, schoolmates and playmates during carefree afternoons in the square amid the housing projects on the edge of the town. They had played capture the flag and dodge ball; in the morning during the first hour of class Adriana copied the homework from the orderly notebooks of a diligent student. Then she had changed, the lines of her body curved, she washed her hair more often and in the light the dark brown shone here and there with flashes of copper. Vittorio's intentions changed as well; the complicity he sought was different, more adult the game he asked of her with his gaze alone, his nostrils flared above the new mustache. Who knows what my sister's life would have been if she had reciprocated. Vittorio would perhaps have taken her far away, where he was going to harness the energy of sun and wind. At least one person in Adriana's class had managed to get his university degree.

"You really don't like him?" I asked her one day.

"He makes me sick, like a brother," she answered then.

That night in the gelato shop Adriana turned and he no longer saw anyone else. He noticed instead the tiny mosquito that was sitting on her shoulder and chased it away with a light gesture, almost a caress.

"Hey, who do you think you are?" and Rafael was immediately on him. He grabbed his rival's shirtfront.

"Leave him alone, he's my cousin," said Adriana and got between the two, facing Rafael, ready to avert the fight but basically proud of being the reason for it. Everyone looked at us and I was silenced by surprise, by an unjustified embarrassment.

"Come on, let's go," I said to Vittorio touching his back.

The ice cream that he hadn't licked was dripping along the cone down to his wrist. Outside he found his group from the town and they left.

Adriana and Rafael also came out, entwined as if nothing had happened, along with Giuditta, still excited by the scene.

I suddenly realized that it was two in the morning: at sixteen my sister was fifty kilometers from home with a man so jealous.

"How will you get home?" I asked her in a whisper.

"Rafael will take me," she answered, unconvinced.

Giuditta invited her to sleep with us, we could all fit in her room, but she didn't want to.

"I'd take a walk with your sister's boyfriend," my friend said, as she closed her eyes.

I stayed awake, thinking.

That might have been Adriana's first night in Borgo Sud, I'm not sure. I know that every so often she went during the day to Rafael's house, where Isolina welcomed her, a little torn between hospitality and suspicion. She was kind in that brisk and genuine way with her son's *guagliona*, but she was also afraid she'd take him away. He was all she had in the world, apart from the big sailing family that in the summer months slept with the doors open. Behind the green house the neighbors gathered on Saturday night to listen to Rafael, who sang, accompanying himself on the guitar. These were moments of happiness for Isolina: her son on land, safe, singing Don Backy's *L'immensità* or our eternal *Vola vola vola*, and the people of Borgo joined in on the chorus. Someone grilled kebabs, someone else passed them around, along with the wine. At the end of the week the men were hungry for meat, they wanted nothing to do with fish, which they'd been scarfing down on the boats for days.

Isolina must have quickly understood that that girl wouldn't take Rafael away, it was she who was seeking a refuge, simple care, protection. She sneaked in among the smells from the stove, the clothes dried in the salt air, the wait for the fishing boats to return from the sea. She went sometimes even when Rafael wasn't there, with the excuse of waiting for him.

"Now you go on up to your mamma," the woman said to her at times.

Maybe they'd all three have lunch together, then she'd go to the neighbor's for a few hours to leave them alone, and on her return she found Adriana still there, who didn't even ask if she had to go home. She seemed an orphan.

I was more orphan than she, but I knew how to hide what was missing. I passed off a false normality. I tied myself to Piero at twenty-five, not too young, but I knew so little of myself. Certain Sundays in winter he and I had no desire even to get up from the couch and go out on the city streets. Our side by side solitudes warmed us to the bone.

8.

In Viale Regina Margherita I slowed down as much as I could. Adriana looked out distracted, her forehead wrinkled, the photograph of our brother on her knees. I had to hurry and speak, at home we'd find Picro with the baby and she wouldn't say anything.

"At least do you know when Rafael will be back?" I asked her cautiously.

She shook her head no, annoyed.

"If you tell me what happened, maybe I can help you."

She shifted, leaning against the door with a hostile expression. She huffed, muttering to herself. Suddenly she leaned toward me, so that her nose was practically touching me.

"You want to help me? How much money do you have? Rafael's in serious debt, if you want to know," and she turned away again, in the other direction, arms folded.

I was silent, after the unexpected lunge.

"Will you stop going at this snail's pace? Maybe it's time for your nephew to be fed," she shouted suddenly. The entire car vibrated with her rage.

I obeyed instinctively, pressing on the accelerator.

"Right now I don't have much," I said, turning onto Via Zara. "I just bought the car and I'm still paying the installments on the furniture," I explained.

"Then you can't help me," she concluded curtly in front of the garage.

In the elevator she seemed to have calmed down, but she had some cold poison in reserve for me.

"If you pay for everything, I don't understand why you married Piero," she said, looking at the buttons.

"I have a job, my husband doesn't have to support me," I said, turning the key in the lock.

In the middle of the afternoon the house was cool, fragrant with the lavender I'd dried the year before. Piero had closed and shuttered the windows facing the sun, opened the others. In summer he controlled the breezes, the shade, so we didn't suffer from the heat. He was in the kitchen with Vincenzo, feeding him yogurt by playing airplane. He had even changed him, an edge of the diaper was sticking out of the garbage can.

The tension of the trip to Borgo Sud suddenly relaxed in nerves and muscles, even the news of Rafael's debts seemed less ominous. I sat on the couch, on the side that kept the imprint of my figure, my sharp elbow. I listened to the voices coming toward me: Piero was describing the hours spent with the baby, Adriana was praising both. From the wall opposite books and pictures gazed at me, the tapestry with mysterious faces under big hats.

Of the houses I'd lived in none had been so much mine, maybe only the one in Montesilvano where I'd grown up with my aunt and uncle, but I didn't know then that I was happy. One morning at the age of thirteen I had awakened in the town, and next to me Adriana had peed. We barely knew each other.

During university I'd found a room with a bathroom and kitchen on the outskirts of Pescara. It had nothing welcoming about it. From there a bus took me to Chieti, for classes, another to the center, where I helped some students with their homework. From the only window you could see a wall, too close, with a drainpipe that went down to a concrete slab. It was broken in one place, so it leaked whenever it rained, and the water stained the yellow wall. Studying I watched the line lengthen into forks and fringes, turn green because of some tiny vegetation that grew on it. This was my only view; not for the hole in the drainpipe I think I would have gone mad in that room.

Adriana came in my second year. She was tired of ruining her hands in the country—she wanted "a clean job in the city."

The first day she came back from the neighborhood super-market with bread and a large jar of lotion to soften her cal-luses and repair the cracked skin. She wasn't in a hurry to look for work, she couldn't show up with those boorish hands, she said. Sitting on the cot I'd opened for her, she spread Nivea, massaging it for a long time. She had never taken such care of herself.

Meanwhile she'd caught Rafael again. They had left each other for months, one of the countless times. I seldom met him, Adriana brought him home only when I wasn't there. Once he forgot a package of condoms in the bathroom and I pretended not to see it, until my sister took it away. She pre-ferred to keep us separate, and see him amid the boats, the sea, and the fish, Isolina and Borgo Sud. In that outlying neighbor-hood of reinforced concrete we were so far from the water that not even a breeze reached us. I never really knew Rafael, and he continues to elude me.

Adriana's untidiness and some of my intolerances kindled furious fights. She'd slam the door and return maybe after two days, since she had that other place to stay. She'd come back to me so that she could go out at night when Rafael was at sea: he wasn't supposed to know that his *guagliona* had fun without him. Adriana ran wild in those years. I couldn't contain her in the dangerous exercise of her freedom.

The carabinieri brought her home one frightening dawn. She had been at the feast of the Madonna of Seven Sorrows since the afternoon, and I hadn't seen her. She joined the more disreputable groups, went to neighborhoods like San Donato and Rancitelli, met people who lived in the Treno or Ferro di Cavallo, including dealers. I still can't explain to myself how she never became an addict, with everything she touched. Adriana is like that: she can be submerged in the muck and she comes out pure.

The carabinieri had found her with certain foolish characters from Zanni who at the end of the glorious evening had gone to the city center to break windows, in her case they had taken only the basic information.

"Keep a closer watch on your sister," said the old corporal, looking at me sleepless and despairing.

Our parents never came to see us in this house, they didn't even know where it was. They said generically that I was—then we were—in Pescara, and they uttered the name as if it were a fabulous, exotic place. The fifty kilometers' distance was multiplied by their deep-rootedness in the town. They trusted me, "as long as we don't have to find the money for you," they said, but even with Adriana they stopped that minimal vigilance that could lead to violent punishment. After she came to live with me they withdrew from her life. "Now you take care of your sister," my father said.

Only the carabinieri scared her, but that didn't last long. For a few days she didn't go out, she reorganized and cleaned, silent, and with the radio off. I almost believed she was working the same way inside herself.

Before my sister arrived I had shared the room and the rent with Linda. From the province of Teramo her parents came to see her with big boxes of provisions: ready-made sauces, jams, mushrooms. They even brought eggs, and bread baked by her mother, still warm in the knotted cloth. I remember precisely the fragrance of the loaves and Linda's generosity when it was her and me. If she invited a boy, however, she wouldn't dream of setting the table for three. She was studying architecture, and there wasn't space in the room for the drafting machine her father bought her, so she left, or maybe it was because of the unbearable weight of my sadness.

At least Adriana and I were equal, left to ourselves, alone in the world, sisters. We fought about the radio being on while I was studying, the window that she wanted open and I closed, what time she got home. For both of us certainty of the other remained at the base of the suffering we never confessed to each other.

Some weekends we went home, not always together, Adriana more infrequently. Then she began working in bars and restaurants, switching often. "Now I have to have a little freedom," she'd say at a certain point, and she'd rest for two or three months, or even longer.

Saturday and Sunday my mother seemed indifferent to my presence. Between laundry and stove she almost never spoke, but she usually cooked what I liked, or at the moment of departure she put in my bag a jar of pickled vegetables.

My mother was always unpredictable. She had unexpected kindnesses, then shut herself in again. I knew those attentions and their intermittence. I tried to win them, but it wasn't for merit or guilt that they arrived or were absent. If I had known that when I was younger, I wouldn't have wasted the effort: if I had known that her affection didn't depend on me.

Adriana asked Odilia for work at the end of a summer. She had spent it making pizzas at a beach club and wanted to cool off, she said. It was a long trip inland, from the coast to a country village with a few houses around a crossroads. The restaurant Al Bivio was closer to the town than to Pescara and it wasn't the cool air that my sister was looking for there.

If memory is still solid on this interminable night, I was coming home from the literary criticism exam. Rafael, just getting off the boat, had arrived at our window on his motorbike, and the scene between inside and outside could be heard as far away as the port, even the fish in the water must have trembled. Someone had told him about Adriana's wanderings during his absences. After his furious outburst he had

left, tires screeching on the old Ciao; she had thought about
it a bit and got a bag ready.

The restaurant was always full, because of the *arrosticini*, the
skewers with large chunks of meat cut by hand. Adriana hus-
tled until late evening, paying no attention to the hours of work,
and most of the time she stayed overnight if she couldn't get a
ride to the town. She was charmed by the place, forgetting for
a moment Borgo and her raging love. In front the restaurant
was like others: a small parking lot, a neon sign, pots of red
geraniums, as I saw when I went there. In the back a wild, mysterious countryside opened up, apart from the enclosure where
Odilia's garden was. Her animals lived free, only the cat slept
in the house. The goat grazed on the tasty bushes along a
nearby drainage ditch. At the same time every morning the dog
barked, and as if at an agreed-on signal the cat with a leap lowered the handle on the inside of the door and let him in. The
goat followed them up the stairs with a sound of delicate high
heels and together they entered Odilia's room. She opened her
blue eyes and looked at them happily. Adriana got up just to
see them and laughed.

Then Rafael felt the usual longing for that nervous body
and that crazy head, and went to eat *arrosticini* at her place.
Someone must have told him where she was.

Adriana didn't want to leave the restaurant, but suddenly it
was too far. She decided to get her license and buy a used car.
When the money wasn't enough she thought of the many
hours of unpaid overtime and simply took it out of Odilia's till.

9.

It all happened in an afternoon.

Odilia left goat, dog, and cat and arrived at the town in the Ape. She consumed the uphill curves, straining the engine to the maximum. She knew the road, the parking area outside the building where the children protested at every car that arrived to take space away from their games. She'd come to pick up Adriana a few times, when she'd missed the bus and at the restaurant there was the meat to put on the skewers. That night she hadn't stayed to sleep at Odilia's, she had left with Rafael and a whispered goodbye. A few days earlier she'd asked for the two or three paychecks in arrears, also bringing up the overtime that was never calculated. Of the girls who had worked there she was the smartest, but also too much, in the end. Certainly she wouldn't have showed up again, after cleaning out the cash register.

But she wasn't home. At the insistent ringing of the bell my mother looked out on the landing, so all the neighbors, resting in the cloudy afternoon heat, also heard Odilia, sweaty and panting. They heard what she came to say about Evuccia's daughter and discussed it for weeks. In the town they still remember Adriana's crime at the Al Bivio restaurant, which no longer exists.

In the time the sun took to disappear behind the Cappuccini, everything reached a crisis. My sister must have arrived shortly before I got off the bus—certainly she had slept in Borgo Sud. I heard the yelling louder and louder as I approached, then I began to distinguish insults and curses, and the word "shame" repeated by the two voices. I flew toward the square, indifferent to the few passersby who stared at me, surprised by that breathless run. My heart was bursting in my chest and I already felt the shame they were shouting. Upstairs there were other sounds, not just cries. I saw them as soon as I went in: slaps, shoves, tugs; a body that fell or crashed against the wall, the table askew, chairs overturned. The clothes that had been brought in and folded lay everywhere on the floor, one bore the dark imprint of a shoe. My mother was hitting Adriana, and that I could believe, but Adriana was also hitting my mother. She bit her arm right before my eyes, before my eyes she thrust a hand in her face with all her strength. I needed some moments to conceive of the scene I was looking at. Then I closed the door and threw myself into the middle of that fury, screaming: that's enough, stop it, leave her alone. Animal claws, nails scratched me, went on fighting because they couldn't stop. They ended it suddenly, their breathing uncontrolled, hot and frantic on me.

When she could, my mother spoke: "Don't say anything to your father, he's coming home now."

She took a step, again to confront Adriana. From the neck of her everyday dress she pulled out her breast, I'd never seen that part of her so intimate, white, shriveled by the hunger of six children. She took it between index and middle fingers, as if in the act of offering it to a nursing child, aimed the purple nipple.

"May you be cursed forever, damned for laying your hands on me. I gave you blood and milk, I curse you."

She stuck her breast back in the dress, straightened a chair, picked up the clothes, and disappeared into her room. Adriana remained immobile, drained, her hair stuck to her pale face. I looked at her, in an inextricable knot of pain and horror.

I don't know for certain which of the two started it. My

sister swore it wasn't her, she had as usual absorbed the insults—thief, whore—and the first slaps. She told me later, we were in bed. Only our father had had dinner, each of us had invented an excuse, headache, stomach ache.

"When she said I'm a dishonor to the family I just couldn't see anymore, I started hitting, too. What sort of family are we?" she asked.

I didn't know how to answer her.

I was afraid of the curse. These were old superstitions, magical thinking and ignorance, I tried to reassure myself, but I was afraid for her.

She resumed her life in Pescara, partly with me, partly in Borgo Sud, working where she found something. I saw that shadow over her and I'm sure that she, too, felt the weight of it.

Some time later, in Adriana's absence, I confronted my mother.

"You should remove the curse. Adriana is your daughter."

She shrugged her shoulders in that way she had of diminishing every subject.

"I don't know how. If your sister doesn't change her ways she'll come to a bad end," she said.

On the night table the telephone vibrates again, slides a little on the surface. I didn't think I'd get an answer to my message of a few minutes ago, I just tossed out a question, a hook in this darkness, this silence, convinced that it wouldn't catch any fish. I'm not the only one awake, it seems. A formal language reports that the circumstances of what happened have not yet been clarified and developments are expected in the next hours. Then it changes tone: *I'll come by the hotel at eight, try to sleep now. You'll see, tomorrow we'll know something.* We're all mistaken, with this tomorrow that is already today.

The temptation to telephone Christophe comes to my fingers, here's the number. I give it up. Here I can't find the nerve. If I were in Grenoble I would cross the landing and knock softly on his door, he says I can do it anytime.

"Hector wanted to come to you," I would apologize.

Sometimes he's already awake at that hour, lost in his notes. Or he didn't sleep at all: there's no way to understand him. His sleep is brief and concentrated. All it takes is a glance for him to know how I am. I sit on a small sofa, covered in colored wool, and he lights the stove, opens the wooden box of tea: sage and lemon is my favorite. For the cat Dano snacks, organic. With the hot cup in my hands and Christophe sitting so calmly opposite, it's easy to confide. He looks at my blue silk pajamas and says I'm elegant even at night. He says little about himself, but he's an attentive listener. He caresses our Chartreux on his lap and listens. He notices the Italian accent that sometimes echoes in my French.

Then Hector opens his yellow eyes and moves to my lap. I feel the warmth of Christophe's hands on the gray fur. He found us right away, after the death of his old mistress on the second floor. She was a woman alone and the cat knew it; he went up to the top step and meowed at Christophe's door. He sniffed the odor of the person who always stopped when he met him on the stairs. I don't know what I wouldn't give to have my neighbor here now.

The day Adriana hit my mother, she insisted that I not say anything to my father, but there was no need. I didn't say it even to myself anymore.

They didn't speak to each other for years, only sullen nods, monosyllables, orders from a twisted mouth—get the pot, clean the floor—the few times that Adriana showed up.

I would have preferred that my sister not go, especially when I wasn't there. I was afraid of what could be repeated. Maybe she was afraid, too, but she went back anyway. She went back to feel she was a daughter, born, alive on the Earth.

This was my family. I returned on Saturday afternoons to

reconnect like Adriana to the same painful root. I never brought anyone from Pescara to the town, not a friend, a boyfriend, not even Piero, for a long time. At the bridge over the Tavo I crossed alone a frontier that divided the world in two.

Sometimes Piero insisted on driving me, and we said good-bye in the square, in front of the gas pump. Rumors about my boyfriend from the city reached the house.

"Why don't you have him come up?" my mother asked.

It was always too soon, even when a ring of white gold shone on my left hand. The day I invited him to dinner the date of the wedding was already set. My father painted the dining room and the kitchen where the paint had peeled off the wall in various places and was stained with grease above the stove. My mother got a set of plates at the Thursday market, otherwise they would have all been different, some a little chipped. It wasn't the white porcelain Piero was used to but they stood out in those shiny colors on the ironed tablecloth and I liked them.

She made *crespelle in brodo*, then a free-range chicken that a farmer woman had brought that morning. I helped her with my eye on the clock, I dropped a potato, a knife. I broke a glass and the fragments scattered everywhere.

A little before Piero arrived there was a squabble for the shower: we both needed it at the same moment, my mother felt she smelled of roast chicken. She asked me to do her hair and I satisfied her, keeping at bay my unease at the unusual closeness of her body.

"You could be a hairdresser," she commented at the end, and who knows what she meant, gratitude, a compliment, the call to a more useful and concrete job.

Nothing I feared happened, Piero ate the crepes and said, licking a finger, that he had never eaten a chicken like that. He talked to my father about his passion for the mountains and the unbearable traffic of Pescara. They understood each other, between the Italian of one and the half adjusted dialect of the other. In turn they poured the wine.

My mother, more silent, went back and forth between table and stove, with her eye on the guest. When they said goodbye he instinctively kissed her on the cheeks.

Later I washed the dishes and she took off the tablecloth. It was then that she said: "He's a fine young man, but it's clear he's not of our kind. He seems a little too much for you."

I turned off the water and looked toward her. Involuntarily she'd strike like that, in cold blood and deeply. Maybe I also felt that Piero was too much for me.

I bit my lip and stopped trembling. Then I answered.

"Remember I grew up somewhere else. And I went to school."

She wasn't impressed for so little, she put in the last word: "If he makes you suffer later, don't come here to cry."

It wasn't the curse hurled at Adriana, but it weighed like a prophecy.

The darkness of Room 405 is illuminated now by a sudden truth: my mother had divined the future of her female children, she had a presentiment in that visceral way of hers, physical, like a colic, an intestinal upset. My mother was in her omens. When Adriana came to me with the baby, when she told me about the debts of her man, she had just that cursed face.

10

The child, laughing at the saleswoman making faces and cooing at him, had deep dimples in his cheeks. With her support, he was sitting on the wooden counter, next to the cash register. The owner observed them in amusement, waiting to hand the dresses she was holding to someone in the dressing room. An arm I knew reached out from behind the curtain to take them. I pretended interest in the items displayed in the window, reading the prices in disbelief—more than three hundred thousand lire for a straight skirt—and meanwhile looked inside.

I had seen Vincenzo by chance. There was Adriana, in a dress with shoulder straps that was light blue over the bosom and descended, shading through all the gradations, to darker blue at the ankle. She looked at herself with satisfaction, turned to see the effect from the back. The woman showed her a jacket to go with it, but she shook her head no. She wanted the dress, however, in an elegant black bag that said "SAN-TOMO." I left before she came out.

I was seething as I headed home: with all the fear she had of being found by whoever it might be, she had gone out shopping to the most famous boutique in the city. She turned onto Via Zara as I opened the entrance door, walking quickly behind the carriage. From a distance, with her hair so short and my dark glasses, she looked like a punk.

"You say you're in debt and then you buy clothes at Santomo?"

I confronted her in the entrance, without giving her time to undo the strap around Vincenzo, pick him up.

"If you want to know, in ten days I have to go to a wedding in Picciano and I can't show up in rags," she said, but she wasn't upset.

At the marriage of Rafael's cousin she would be the bride's witness. Her voice broke at his almost certain absence.

"Why doesn't he come back?" I asked, impatient.

"He's in Morocco, transoceanic fishing," she said.

For two months his boat had been sitting in the port; he'd left to try to make more money. At times Adriana's truths arrived unexpectedly, in bits and pieces.

"At least for the dress you can help, can't you? He'll pay you back at Christmas," she promised, as if she were sure of winning the lottery.

At the shop she'd left a down payment, my telephone number, and, most important, Piero's last name, one of the best known in the city.

"You have no shame," I shouted at her, grabbing my purse.

I left in a fury and before the store closed I paid her debt with a check. To that girl who was so nice she had given the sale price in advance, the woman said, bracelets clanking. You must be kidding, I would have liked to respond as I wrote six hundred thousand next to lire, breathing in her perfume. I warned her against giving credit to my sister.

"She likes designer dresses, but she can't afford them. I won't pay for her anymore."

Taking her aside, I also asked her not to say anything to Piero's mother, one of her best customers.

I limited to the minimum the contact between my parents and the Rosati family, they must have met on two or three occasions around the time of the wedding. My parents were harmless, they lived peacefully in the town, beyond an imaginary line of demarcation. They had no desire to cross the bridge over the Tavo, no interest in the city or the sea. They had never been on a beach, they watched swimmers in bathing suits on television with a sort of pity.

My sister, on the other hand, was a danger, her eccentric routes might take her anywhere. I was afraid that Costanza would find out too much about her, so reckless.

"Don't tell your family that Adriana and the baby are here—it's just for a short time," I warned Piero.

I didn't tell him about the dress with the real shells encrusted on the bodice, of his last name used as a guarantee to have it. He complimented her when he saw it on her, the morning of the wedding.

"I gave it to her," I lied, only in part.

Adriana is an opportunist by instinct, not by calculation. She makes use of those who can be useful to her, preserving a kind of innocence, a childlike candor. She understands that you can use her in the same way.

I don't remember how long after this she went to the bank to ask for a loan, specifying Piero as the guarantor. She told the bank officer to prepare the papers, Doctor Rosati would come by to sign them.

Rafael's debts were hers, fixed in her mind, a black hole that sucked up her energy. She wasted years in search of money. It also took me some time to learn to say no to her. Then she asked Piero, secretly. That he was no longer my husband was for her an insignificant detail.

"He's separated from you, not from me," she answered with ironclad logic when I found out.

Maybe at this hour I could take some more Sédatif PC. I wouldn't count on sleeping anymore, but it might help me face the day tomorrow. Which for hours has already been today. I go to the window for a moment, look at this rectangle of a city that's so American. Every time I come back I find something new. Pescara is a gym for architects and artists. We loved it, my sister and I, each in her own way. It welcomed us. If she hadn't wasted her talent for drawing she could have designed the mirrored train station, the Ponte del Mare, the goblet-shaped fountain in Piazza Salotto. I swallow the capsules without water.

Adriana and the baby were at our house when it happened the first time: Piero didn't come home to sleep. All night I imagined an accident. I took an anti-anxiety pill, I was using Tavor at the time. The pill didn't help, I kept going back and forth between bedroom and kitchen, in a corridor of anguish. I saw the details, the twisted smoking metal, the motor oil dripping on the asphalt. And Piero dead, his beauty untouched in the light of the flashers.

The next morning was Sunday, Adriana came out to the balcony barefoot in the dress she had worn to the wedding the week before. The breeze stirred it in waves from her hips down, a ribbon of sea. Clinging to his mother's neck, Vincenzo, naked, tried to pull a shell off the bodice. They were the picture of summer, of life.

"You dress like that for breakfast??" I asked, fascinated in spite of myself.

"Can't you see what a beautiful day? I want to celebrate it," she said, moving the baby's fingers away from the shell. "And then I want to take advantage, with everything you paid for," and she spun around to show me the splendor of the fabric swelling in the breeze.

"Where's Piero?" she asked, sipping coffee.

"He called a little while ago—he stayed in Rome after the conference."

"He could have made the effort to call you last night, you have horrible bags under your eyes."

"He decided late and didn't want to wake me," I said darkly from my wicker chair.

She reflected a little, as if holding something back.

"Your husband must be the best dentist in Italy to go to all these conferences," she said then.

Piero didn't leave that suspicion time to touch me, he arrived while we were still sitting there, in front of the empty cups. I didn't get up to greet him, I think I even moved aside when he bent over to hug me and apologize, offering as many apologies as the kisses on my hair. He brought *cornetti* from Renzi and a present for me from the capital: hand-crafted silver earrings with little corals. The night just passed seemed like a nightmare that I could almost forget. Adriana looked at him shrewdly, silent, in her billowing dress.

It happened again, later. He had been working for a short time with an office in Foggia, where he went once a week. He told me not to worry if he didn't come home at night: better to sleep in the place after a day of work. Did I remember that fit of drowsiness on the highway, two years ago? He had been saved by a miracle.

I didn't worry. Today I have trouble recognizing myself in the accommodating wife I was. I was stubborn in my patience.

We were supposed to go on an outing to the Maiella that day, but the others had already left.

"Then I'll take you to the beach—not right here, though, let's go to Torre di Cerrano," Piero proposed, anxious to repay me.

Adriana suddenly reached for the sunglasses on the table and put them on. I saw precisely the dark flash of her gaze on him, an instant before she covered it.

We went on the motorbike, speeding along the coast. I held onto him tight to stay in the seat. After years together, a cramp in my stomach, of desire, still surprised me. Every so often he let go of the handlebars and caressed my arm.

There weren't many people on the beach at Torre. We stretched out on our backs on adjacent towels. A plover came running toward us amid the dunes, followed by its chicks, already partly grown. We hadn't seen the nest in the sand, a few meters away. They crouched in the hole and the little ones sheltered under the maternal wings, in the thicker and softer feathers. I whispered my amazement to Piero, but he barely looked at them. He got up suddenly.

I went to the shore and he was already distant, swimming steadily and swiftly, crossing the strips of color of the water. In a few minutes his head became a dark point in the blue. I swam by myself.

"Nice weather in Hvar?" I joked when he returned to the towels.

"Raining," and he let his hair drip on my back.

"Yesterday Morelli called, he invited us for a couple of days to his house in Scanno. In September he's assigning me an important seminar, and I can choose a writer of the twentieth century myself."

Piero was pleased: he had always predicted a brilliant career for me. Of himself he said on every occasion that he had been a mediocre student, that he wouldn't have celebrated his degree if he hadn't met me.

"I want to suggest Pavese, but as a poet. 'Death will come and will have your eyes,' remember?"

My first gift to him, on a warm May evening. He had been a little bewildered by the title: with the slim book in his hand he looked now at me, now at the cover. It must have seemed to him not a gift but a presentiment. I carried those pages embodied in a profound memory, and didn't even know why. I found in every line the improbability of love, then Piero had arrived to deny it.

We had met a few weeks before, on the steps of the D'Annunzio university. He was sitting with a grim face, a textbook open upside down a few steps below.

"You dropped this," I had said, holding it out to him.

In fact the book had been flung down after another failure on the dental restoration exam. He took it back out of politeness.

"Do you feel like a coffee? Maybe it will cheer me up."

The boys I had known faded instantly. It had begun like that. At the same time Morelli was waiting for me in his office to talk about my doctoral thesis.

I turned, Piero was asleep, drying in the sun. The plovers had left their nest, scurrying over the sand.

He woke suddenly, maybe from a dream. He looked around disoriented, recognized the Torre, me beside him.

We had lunch at Cerrano Sub, the closest beach club. We knew the old owner, very thin and tan in all seasons. He cooked pennette with clams and fresh tomatoes, then grilled fish. With bread we mopped up the sauce, which tasted of the sea.

I didn't ask him anything that day, he poured white wine and clinked my glass with his. I drank, reassured.

Piero was surrounded by a sort of magnetic field that in the years of our marriage repelled my anger, excluded certain questions, generated misunderstandings. I never completely reached him in his separateness, never in his truth. I was afraid to push beyond appearances, calm as the water beyond the dunes of Cerrano.

11

We escaped the city on the motorbike, on a gray morning. In the Gole del Sagittario we felt a coolness we'd missed for months, I shivered in the patches of shade.

"Let's go see this famous professor," Piero had said.

I didn't think he would immediately agree to go with me to Scanno. He yawned sometimes when I talked with the enthusiasm of the devoted student.

Morelli was waiting for us in the town square, with the paper under his arm. He was wearing a blue polo shirt instead of the usual dark suit and he smiled through his neat beard. We had never met outside of the university, he shook my hand with a new warmth. I introduced my husband.

"But we've met in Pescara, at the tennis club," he said, looking at him closely.

Piero had taken up tennis again the year before. The mountains weren't enough for his need for activity, for hard work. At the club he relaxed after a day spent leaning over the mouths of patients, he said. He thought about it for a moment, he didn't remember seeing the professor.

"Don't worry, I come every so often to watch a few matches, but I've stopped treading the courts. You play with Davide Ricci, the son of my friend the engineer. He's got that athlete's physique—he's strong, Davide, eh?"

Piero didn't answer. Then they talked about cups and tournaments, red clay or grass, while we walked amid the stone houses. I listened in silence, I had never gone to a match, or asked him if he had won or lost. I didn't know who he played with. Only the outfit that he put in the washing machine fell to my hands.

"Here in '57 Giacomelli took the famous photograph that was shown at MoMA," the professor said, stopping at a view.

"*Scanno Boy*," I recalled.

"Yes. The child walking with his hands in his pockets and an adult gaze, the only subject in focus among the women, who are all in black," and Morelli turned three-quarters to me. "Also Cartier-Bresson worked on these streets, and Berengo Gardin."

He indicated the marvels of the town, as if he were pointing to the blackboard during a class. "But before them," he added, touching my arm, "a woman came, Hilde Lotz Bauer, in the thirties."

"So you know about photography, too, not only tennis and literature," Piero said, a step behind us.

Morelli turned toward him, leaving his irony suspended for a moment. He said hello to a man who, meeting us, greeted him with respect.

"As our Flaiano says, today even the fool has a specialty. I prefer to keep my eyes open to the world," he said then.

Piero's unhappiness reached me like electricity in the air. He was pondering something, maybe he felt excluded.

Signora Nina greeted us at the house, which was furnished with care and few concessions to the rustic: wood-paneled walls, a stone hearth that occupied an entire side of the living room. She wore a floral perfume and was warm from standing at the stove. The only indulgence in her refined simplicity were the *circeglie,* the classic boat-shaped Scannese earrings that dangled from her earlobes.

"Here you are, finally. He's been talking about you since you were his student."

She ignored the hand I held out and hugged me. I would

hear her refer to her husband always with that pronoun, a he that sounded capitalized, like an *ipse*. I had imagined them just like that: they passed the water or the bread, and the habit of tenderness leaked out from every gesture. They weren't distracted by children; they had none.

We had lunch in a luminous kitchen, the two open windows seemed like paintings of the lake, of the woods, I sat opposite the professor, Piero beside me. He was eating tagliatelle with porcini when suddenly he stopped. Out of the corner of my eye I saw him put his fork down and not move.

"What's happened? Are you full?" Morelli asked.

"I'm sorry, I don't eat mushrooms," Piero lied.

"A moment ago you were eating them eagerly," the other immediately resumed.

"Then excuse me, but with this hair on the plate I can't finish." We looked and there was a hair of Nina's, dyed brown, capriciously twisted around a noodle. She got up and stood staring at it, her palms tense on the edge of the table. She repeated no, shaking her head mechanically, in an uncontrollable way, her earrings sounding like agitated bells.

"Calm down, Nina, it happens," said her husband, touching her arm and leading her gently to sit down.

"Don't worry, I'll happily eat the second course," Piero reassured her.

Morelli's gaze didn't leave him.

No one had an appetite now, the professor and I twirled the pasta with unwilling forks. His wife made an effort for a moment, then gave up. I don't recall how long it was before that conspicuous trembling of her head stopped.

"It was really wonderful," I said at the end, my face still red.

I didn't look at Piero. He complimented the roast, and the second helping he almost insisted on perhaps restored Nina's good will, but not Morelli's. He couldn't forgive him for having exposed her in her fragility.

"So you are a dental technician," he said, spearing a new potato.

"A dentist," Piero explained. No one could know the difference better than a university professor, but the skirmish continued, with other requests for clarification. On the motivation for becoming a dentist, for example. Was it a career one chose out of an unlikely vocation or a desire for money? Piero began to get impatient and agitated in his chair, I was sweating. I placed a hand on his tense leg, under the tablecloth. He shifted it, abruptly. He said that someone had to do the dirty work.

"You continued the profession of your father, I know him by reputation. But he's a doctor," Morelli insisted.

He sniffed the berry pie that was served, still warm, by Nina, who had cheered up. He scratched his cheek with a prickly sound.

"I chose a shorter degree course instead—I didn't want to waste all those years on books," Piero provoked him.

I was afraid that at that point Morelli would chase him out of a vacation house whose walls were nevertheless lined with valuable volumes. I was also afraid of losing his respect, which that day had been displayed more affectionately, far from the gray classrooms of the university. He looked at me, and said nothing.

He lowered his tone, allowed himself a last remark: "I understand that to give up an activity initiated by a parent requires a certain courage."

Piero opened his mouth to respond, closed it a moment later. He was molding the white of the bread with his fingertips, reducing it to a ball. The warning signs I had felt in the town square were transformed into an intense stomach ache. I excused myself and went to the bathroom. Sitting on the edge of the tub I bent forward, holding my breath. The linen towels with the embroidered initials, the blue soap, the baroque bottle half full of Nina's perfume spun around in my vertigo. Though I strained my ears I couldn't hear the voices in the other room anymore. I was unsure whether to consider it a frightening sign or reassuring. I lifted the lid of the toilet barely in time to throw up that unfortunate lunch.

I was in a hurry to get back to them. I washed out my mouth and took a Spasmomen from my purse.

Nina asked if I was all right. They had gone into the living room for coffee. They seemed tranquil, all three. I looked at Piero in another way. This had never happened, I had never been ashamed of him. Maybe it was what the professor wanted, after all.

Infected by an obscure contagion, for several hours I shifted to his point of view. My husband changed inside me. When we met he was ready to give up his studies, he was already two years behind. We studied for some exams together: I remember the pages with the impressive images of tumors in the oral cavity. He repeated them to me at night, in bed at his country house, between kisses. And Angle's classifications, which he couldn't manage to memorize: "In Class I malocclusions the mesiobuccal cusp of the upper first molar occludes in the mesial groove of the lower first molar."

That day in Scanno I discovered the embarrassment he felt toward an authoritative person and life in general. With the assurance of a solid family behind him, he was more insecure than I.

The empty cups on the table, the spoons next to them. No one spoke. Morelli, palm open, gave a muffled smack to the arm of the chair, like a signal to leave the stall.

"I imagine you also came to ask me about the seminar," he said.

"I'll take advantage of that for a walk on the lake," and Piero jumped up.

In that movement his body became for a moment the center

of the room, illuminated it. The professor offered him his bicycle with the same politeness he'd shown when we arrived that morning. I watched Piero leave, without recognizing the relief I felt.

Morelli's study smelled of paper and wood. He returned to the other room to get his glasses. There was only a table, with a chair behind and one in front for a possible guest. On a shelf of the floor-to-ceiling bookcase volumes on the history of Scanno, on transhumance, on the Tratturo Magno were lined up.

"You can open it," the professor said, indicating an old file I was looking at.

It contained pencil designs by Nina's father, one of the best known Scannese goldsmiths. On paper from Fabriano he had sketched the *presentose*, traditional heart-shaped pendants, the *amorini,* little cupid earrings, the boat-shaped earrings like the ones she was wearing.

We talked about the organization of the seminar, I reminded him it was the first time I'd done this and I didn't know where to begin.

"You can start with Pavese's *Lavorare stanca* and trace the influence of American literature, but don't limit yourself to Whitman, it would be taken for granted. At least consider Steinbeck and Faulkner and also think of the cinema: Keaton and Chaplin," he said.

"I hope I won't disappoint you," I answered, a little fearful.

"Forget unhappy love, it's stuff for freshmen. And a final recommendation: don't work the whole month of August. Think of having some fun."

He gestured vaguely toward the window, the lake, Piero pedaling along the shore, far from us.

Perhaps no one really wanted it, but we had said we would stay overnight. That evening Nina took us to the room she had gotten ready for us on the upper floor, with a view of the two moons, the full one in the sky, the other grainy on the water. The rest was the dark profile of the mountain.

When I came out of the bathroom wearing my bathrobe, Piero was still there, looking out. All my rage deflated in an instant. I embraced him damp from behind, the terrycloth belt came undone on its own.

He loosened my hands from his chest, turning furiously.

"What a great idea to come here today," he began.

"You started it, I don't know why you were so rude to the professor. And not to mention the hair, later."

"You think I should have eaten it?"

I retied the belt. He could have covered it and found a better excuse not to finish the tagliatelle, I said. Instead he had behaved as if he were at his house, with his mother who always indulged him. He had embarrassed everyone.

"All your professor wanted was an excuse to put me in a bad light. And you didn't waste a word for me." He turned away again. "You don't respect me, it's obvious," he added.

"Maybe it's you who underestimate yourself."

"The truth is," he said, "that it wasn't clear which side you were on."

"Are you jealous?"

"Me jealous of that windbag? Your idol, the intellectual full of himself?"

I didn't answer. He, too, shut himself up in silence.

That night I lay awake, as now in this hotel room. I see myself and Piero in the bed with the fine linens, turned back to back. He didn't sleep, either. It was almost dawn when from the woods came the anguished cry of a hunted animal.

We left after breakfast, with an excuse, giving up a walk on the path from which the lake appears heart-shaped.

"Say hello to Davide," Morelli said to Piero, who was already on the motorbike.

12.

There's not much left of the night. The window is still a dark rectangle, but the odor of a new day filters through. I can get up. My balance when I first stand up is unsteady. Yesterday all I ate was crackers on the train, and last night I drank the milk that the fair-haired waitress brought up to me. The cup is on the shelf, white and empty, biscuits next to it, on the plate. I bite one, the spasm in my jaw muscles is strong, they're unused to chewing. I leave it. We're so quick to forget what's necessary to keep us alive.

I go down in the elevator, the clerk hears footsteps and composes himself behind the desk. We exchange just a glance and a nod of good morning. The clock on the wall hasn't even reached four-thirty. Outside, the dark lit by the neon of the street lamps welcomes me, and I walk rapidly along the deserted sidewalk, huddling in my jacket. The dampness of the autumn sea clings to me, it's in my lungs as I breathe. I remember a bar near the port that never closes. At first it's just a light in the distance, I head for it.

My table isn't clean, but now I've sat down; a sticky wake runs across it. The sole customer is snoring in the middle of the bar, he looks like a sailor and must have spent the night here, collapsed on the formica counter. A man in a gray sweater comes in, looks at me for a moment, surprised by someone so foreign and so early at the fishermen's café. He shakes the sailor, sits down facing him. The other pulls himself up with the slow movements of someone who's had a lot to drink and tries to straighten his neck. The other orders two *caffè corretti* with rum, observes me furtively.

"Did you hear about that accident that happened?" mutters the drunk.

"What had to happen happened."

I leave some coins with the barman and go out in a hurry. I get to the pier. I need air. Adriana brought me here that summer, I remember the exact point where she stopped. I don't know who had given her the news; she'd been going to the beach every day with Vincenzo. It was very near from the house, sometimes she secured her son to her chest with a colored band and didn't even take the stroller.

"You have to come to the port with me, quick," she said one afternoon, returning at three.

There she is, clear in memory: in pareu and flip-flops running in a diagonal along the dock, toward the moored boats. Here she suddenly fell to her knees, beating her fist against that bollard that had no line attached to it. She looked at the empty space in the water, small murky waves feebly licked the concrete jetty under her legs. I was behind her, carrying the baby. I don't remember ever having seen her so desperate. She was crying as if the disappearance of Rafael's boat were hers.

She always defended him, excused him, covered up for him. How many times Rafael skipped out on his debts and the creditors came looking for her. Just a few years ago she confided to me the threats, the traps, and I don't know if she told me everything. The night she fled Borgo, One-Eyed Santino had mutilated her hair with a blade, after first running it over her neck.

I, too, believed in the orphaned son of a fisherman who fought for his own redemption. A somewhat delusive fable. My sister was in love with a man with curly black hair who couldn't hold on to a boat called Isolina, like his mother. She was in love with the dream of Rafael, living on the sea with no masters but the wind.

The man in the gray sweater comes out of the bar and goes off with that scythelike gait. Suddenly I remember it: I recognize Antonio. How he's changed, but that way of moving his legs is the same. He was so young then, fifteen years have gone by. I've changed, too, or he only pretended not to recognize me. I could have talked to him, while he was having coffee with the drunk. Now it's too late, he's already disappeared around the corner.

That day Adriana dried her tears with the back of her hand and headed straight toward the metallic sounds that could be heard over where the women of Borgo put up the stalls. The first one who saw her passed on the news, in a moment they had left the cart, or the sawhorses, and hurried to her, in their aprons. They hugged her and touched her short hair, they looked at her to believe she had really appeared on the dock at the port channel.

"Where were you hiding?" a pregnant girl they called Rosita asked.

They also saw me and Vincenzo, he let them hold him without fear, as if every face were known, as if those hands had already caressed him.

"Who took the boat? Is it possible you don't know anything?" Adriana asked one, then another.

"Wait till the men come, maybe they've heard something," said Rosita. She passed the back of her index finger over Vincenzo's round cheek, thinking perhaps of her baby.

I think my annoyance at the intimacy between the two, that talk so free, so familiar, was jealousy. My sister had replaced me with new affections.

A siren like the squawk of a goose announced that the first fishing boat was entering the port. In a moment the women had dispersed in the direction of their stalls and opened the big umbrellas; one bathed the asphalt with a rubber hose and steam rose into the air.

"Come here, you can't stay in the sun," Rosita said. "You, too," she added, looking at me, who had remained a few steps back. Between her upper incisors she already had deep cavities, you could see. Piero would have intervened immediately with some fillings.

Rosita sheltered us in her blue shade, and from there we followed the boat's maneuvers as it entered the harbor, its wake trailing.

Adriana went over to the boat, the Limaflò. With whistles and gestures she asked the fishermen to throw her the line and she secured it to a bollard. Like the roughest of sailors, she knotted the rope, tugging at it, without sparing her skin. I could see where she got the calluses and cracks on her palms.

"Get away with those professor hands of yours," she still says now when there's a dirty job or heavy things to lift.

On board men in yellow boots up to their chests were moving around. Adriana turned to Rosita's husband, it was his boat. Him, Antonio.

"I need to talk to you now, hurry up," she shouted at him from the dock and he answered with a nod.

Then she started unloading the chests so furiously that a long cod fell to the ground. A fisherman handed them to her and she arranged them on the stall, while from the other direction someone was already approaching to choose the fish laid out by type, in rows on the polystyrene like dead soldiers.

Rosita weighed them and put them in the sacks, took the money from the customers with damp fingers. Then Adriana helped her, while alongside the men were loading the wholesaler's van.

"No need to wash them, tap water ruins them," my sister said to a woman as she wrapped some small squids.

She suspended one in the air, swung it for a moment, holding it by a fin, and ate the whole thing. She chewed convincingly, a tentacle hung from her lips.

I turned away in disgust and when I looked at her again she had opened an oyster and offered it to Vincenzo's curious tongue. I wasn't quick enough to move him, and in my arms the boy licked the sticky salty taste of the sea.

Antonio finished loading the van and came into the shade. He ran his hand over Rosita's tensed belly, in a rough caress. My sister said something to him in an undertone and they walked out along the dock, speaking against the sun, up to that bollard.

"Those cowards, they made their raid just now when Rafael's not here," I heard her say before their voices moved out of earshot.

They returned quickly, since there was nothing to see, only the boat's empty spot.

"They'll bring it back if they get their money. We're looking to collect something among the fishermen, but it'll be a nothing," Antonio whispered.

He spread his arms to measure an impotence.

"Adria', you know that in Borgo we're all one family," he responded to her thanks.

The blazing heat of the day diminished, the women piled up the empty chests, they took down the stalls with the help of brothers and husbands exhausted by the sea. Shoo, shoo, you gulls, shouted a boy chasing away the seagulls that had landed in search of remains.

I was not so far from my house, and yet it was completely different, a world apart. There I had left a small book open to poems I loved, a seminar to prepare, an established order; here, where Adriana had brought me, life seemed truer, pulsing and terrible. I was drawn to it and frightened by it at the same time.

Adriana took the child back, Rosita gave me the bag she'd prepared for us. She had tied the handles, inside something alive was wriggling.

Her belly of six or seven months made something of an impression, in her still adolescent body. I asked her how old she was.

"Almost nineteen," she said, convinced that it wasn't so young.

Like my mother in her first pregnancy. I imagined her like Rosita, still thin but already scarred by work, and all those children ahead. I wanted to shake the girl, tell her to stop in that drift. I saw for a moment her future: a tired woman with too many children. I would have liked to shout at her my pity and a mistaken rage. Instead I wrote the number of Piero's office on a piece of paper, my husband could fix her teeth, I said.

"You're leaving? You won't come by to say hello?" Antonio asked, looking Adriana straight in the face.

It was so clear whom he was talking about. She turned toward me for a moment, undecided.

"I'll go with you. With what's happening you can't go two women and a baby," Antonio said.

Then he set off, sure of being followed. He still wore the T-shirt and pants from the sea, they gave off a scent of salt and fish. He had taken off only his yellow boots.

The first time we had entered from the back of the house, but I recognized it from the green of the plaster. Sautéing garlic aggressively invaded the street. Of the two doors only one was closed and beside the other was Isolina on a plastic chair. She stared at the street with small blue eyes, her lips contracted. Her hair seemed dried out by faded dye and a permanent that was too stiff. Two centimeters of white at the roots measured the time that had passed since the last coloring.

She didn't see us right away. Antonio approached first.

"Look who I brought you, Isoli'," he said softly.

She withdrew suddenly from her thoughts, raised her head abruptly. Vincenzo recognized her, flew to her arms. She kissed him for a long time, bathing him with joy. Only afterward did she think of the rest of us; a glance reassured her of Adriana's health. A cordial good evening for me, the most unconnected. The smell of garlic was turning bitter, as of a pan forgotten on the stove. From a window opposite came a voice: "Isoli', what are you burning?"

Adriana ran to the kitchen to turn off the stove and we all went in behind her. We sat around the table, in the bitter smoke that slowly dissipated. The room was the same and symmetrical to the one I had seen with my sister on the other side, when we came to get her things. On the walls were sacred images, a dried, dusty olive branch was attached to the side of a Sant'Andrea with the blessing bleached to invisibility.

"Adria', in the fridge there's some bottles of Gingerino and also get the wafers," Isolina said. "My head is going mad with all these troubles," she added, waving the stink of burning away from Vincenzo with her free hand.

Antonio emptied a bottle and ate two wafers before leaving. With his foot he reattached a piece of baseboard that had come unglued from the wall. He would wait outside to escort us again, out of there.

Isolina caressed her grandson, whom she'd sat in front of her on the table. She looked at the child intensely, certainly she was reading his father's features.

"My poor son, he's always got bad luck. I hope they drop dead," she muttered at a certain point.

Without ever naming him, she, my sister, and Antonio had been talking about a loan shark with the cops after him.

None of us breathed, not even the grandmother was reacting to Vincenzo's babbling anymore. Adriana stood up, and Isolina took her arm.

"When Rafael comes back he'll have plenty of money. We'll

get the boat. And you can come back here," and she indicated with her head the other half of the house.

Then she turned to me, more formal: "For the moment thank you. Soon they can come back here," she repeated.

Antonio must have heard her, from the door.

"With what he brings from Africa, Rafael won't begin to pay even the interest. Isolina doesn't understand that," he said to us outside.

Isolina died three or four years ago, in time to be spared some pain. Until the last day she invested her pension in an attempt to cover her son's debts. If she were still there I would extend my walk to the green house, a few minutes from here. She used to get up so early I could knock on the door and have her coffee.

13.

We left in silence, oppressed by the weight of Antonio's words. Ahead of us on the road along the sea was a convertible driven by a blonde with a white silk scarf around her neck. When she accelerated, the ends fluttered in the air, iridescent—as if she were in a movie, with those slender arms and flying hair. The capriciousness of memory recovers such a negligible detail in this morning that's still dark.

"But he's kind, your friend," I said, turning toward Adriana.

She was looking out at the beach, deserted at sunset, and the darkening blue of the water. She hadn't seen the blonde ahead of us and anyway wouldn't have cared.

"In Borgo kindness doesn't exist, Antonio is a brother," she answered when I'd stopped expecting it.

He and Rafael had grown up together, together in school and street games, running off to sea after struggling to get their middle school diplomas. They were sleeping next to each other on a boat rammed accidentally by a Turkish ship, on a moonless night off Ortona. Rafael had pulled out his unconscious comrade, delivered him to the outstretched hands of the rescuers. Some of the blood that painted Antonio's back had remained on his arms, mingling with the blood of his wounds, which were less serious.

Adriana told me this along the shore, and about Minuccio, who acted as a father to Rafael, too, orphaned of his own.

It was already dark in the apartment on Via Zara, the days were getting shorter. Vincenzo was complaining, hungry and tired. At the last spoonfuls of grated apple his head dangled sleepily.

Then in the kitchen Adriana grabbed a pair of scissors, opened and closed them several times to see how sharp they were. In the bag that Rosita had given me nothing was moving anymore. My sister, who at the age of ten had never even seen a fish, cleaned them skillfully, with a savage grace in her gestures. She notched the skin of the sole in an exact point and skinned it with an angry rip. Cuttlefish ink sprayed her cheek while she was cutting it up, and dripped down like a black tear.

She cooked with the simplest ingredients: oil, garlic, parsley. She added the fish to the pan in sequence, according to the cooking time. The boat seemed to have disappeared even from her thoughts. Adriana has always been like that, she changes mood from minute to minute, lightly.

"Set the table in there," she said to me, knowing that Piero preferred to eat in the dining room.

But he didn't show up; no one answered at the office at that hour, and he hadn't been seen at the tennis club. Adriana had turned off the flame, she was walking back and forth with her arms folded and her patience long gone. At ten she lighted the stove again and we sat across from each other. She devoured her portion, even the bones of the anchovies. I dawdled with my fork, worried about Piero.

"Eat, nothing's happened to him," said Adriana with her mouth full.

She swallowed and then cleared her throat.

"But this time, when he comes back, ask him what he's up to. Don't be quiet anymore."

I nodded my head yes, she was right. Confronting Piero had become urgent. Something was burning at the center of my chest, a lighted point that was spreading in a circle. My tongue appreciated on its own account the dinner that Adriana had made.

"Who taught you to cook like that?" I asked her as I was finishing.

"Isolina."

A fish scale shone in the middle of her forehead, like a third eye.

Later she went to bed, and I, too, went to my room. I took Lorenzo Mondo's essay on Pavese, with the pencil between the pages, but I knew I wouldn't be able to concentrate. I always started again in the same place, finally I gave up. As I did every evening of that August, I read instead two or three poems from the slim white book. They were my prayers: "Your eyes/will be a vain word,/a tacit cry, a silence."

I turned out the light and lay awake waiting for Piero. Outside the wind was rising. Beside me phosphorescent minutes moved across a clock face, very slow the hours.

I had no reason to think something had happened to him, he wasn't climbing a sixth-degree wall, he wasn't traveling in a car. I stretched out my hand onto his side of the bed: it was empty by choice. I could say the exact time on the clock when for the first time I imagined him with a woman different from me.

He came home at ten after five. My senses, on the alert, picked up every attempt he made not to make noise: he closed the entrance door softly, he used the second bathroom, which was farther away, he came barefoot into the bedroom. I glimpsed his profile seeking the way in the imperfect darkness, touching the furniture in order not to run into it. His odor carried a distance of smoke, of alcohol not entirely covered by toothpaste. I wanted to turn the light on him, but something in his movements stopped me, like a painful weight on my back.

"Where were you?" I asked.

He paused with a start at the foot of the bed, a step back and he found the wall. He leaned his hands against it. In the first hint of day I couldn't read his face. He remained there, like a thief caught by surprise. He was truly stealing a piece of life.

"At dinner with the tennis group. I didn't remember, Davide called at the last minute," he said.

I sat up, every single muscle contracted.

"Why didn't you let me know? Adriana cooked fish for us."

He used the excuse that the restaurant's telephone was broken, but he was aware himself of its insubstantiality. He turned silent in the middle of the sentence, moved an arm vaguely in the air and let it go, so that it fell against his leg.

"I'm sorry, I didn't mean to keep you awake," and he sat on the bed, on the corner closest to me. He squeezed my foot under the sheet and the tension in my leg released reflexively.

"It's happened other times, you only have to tell me. Don't you think I'm expecting you?"

He didn't answer, from his mouth came only confusion.

"Where did you have dinner?" I asked when the unease became unbearable.

"At the Osteria del Leone," he said.

It was our favorite restaurant, at the Colli. We'd order an extravagant number of antipasti, varying according to the season. Piero reserved in advance a small separate room with a single table for two. In the middle was a candle and fresh flowers, in the window the lights of the city rolled toward the sea and the port, up to where I am now. He chose the wine, a white Valentini for our birthdays. On the day itself he liked us to toast alone at the Osteria, with a small cake, and on Sunday there was the obligatory birthday lunch with his parents.

In the delayed light of dawn, the memory of our dinners at the Colli already had the aftertaste of things lost.

"We haven't been going there," I said.

Maybe I was expecting a promise, that he would reserve the room for that Saturday or the week after, at most. Piero was there, silent, folded over himself. The mattress transmitted to me the light vibration of his breath, the blood circulating in his body. Suddenly he brought his hand to his forehead and began to cry, shaking his head in almost mute sobs. Immobilized by my surprise, I watched his tears fall.

After a few moments he went out of the room, as if he needed air. Waiting, I prepared the question, but he didn't come back from the bathroom. I heard his shoes in the hall and then the click of the lock, the entrance door shut. I hadn't been able to keep him.

I watched him from the balcony as he left behind me and the building, the street and sidewalk of the evening stroll. Outside now it was light. He was walking on the beach in the direction of the water, of the clouds thickening along the horizon. For a moment I was afraid that he would continue into the waves, the yellow foam of sand. He stopped at the edge, his eyes on the invisible shore on the other side.

I looked at Piero and the solitude of his footprints. I couldn't find a beginning in what was happening to us. I had erased all the signs, ignored a series of gentle denials, polite irritations. At night in bed I had believed in weariness every time, facing his back.

In a loud voice I called him in the quiet gray of the early morning. He couldn't hear me, but a window opened on the fifth floor, a voice protested from the third. Some residents stared at me from above, they didn't know anything about us.

I went back inside, shivering in my summer pajamas. In the house that his parents had bought for the newlyweds we had been, the furniture, the paintings, plates and glasses separated before we did: those which relatives had given to Piero, those which were mine. The objects had decided, we would take much longer to divide one life from the other. At that moment I wasn't ready to exist in a future different from his. I never have been completely, not even later, or today. Still disbelieving, I tolerate the distance I wanted. I've remained faithful to a man who couldn't love me. It's my secret, my devotion.

I wandered through the rooms and the hall, unable to stop. Sometimes I thought of not seeing him anymore, at others my husband in tears on the edge of the bed seemed to me only a nightmare in the sleep before dawn.

He didn't come back. From the window, the beach with the closed umbrellas and a piece of a log carried by the waves. In their room Adriana and Vincenzo were sleeping; holding on to the handle of the door that I had opened slightly I looked at them. He happy in his cradle, the breath passing through his open lips with a slight hiss. She with her head sunk in the pillow, the strap of her undershirt fallen over her arm. The temptation to wake her was brief, overwhelming. Adriana didn't need another weight, she already had hers.

The painful point that had appeared in my chest the night before pulsed all the way to my nails, to the roots of my hair. I remembered a Sunday in summer, the day of my fourteenth birthday. We had gone to the river on foot with Vittorio and some town boys, we were jumping on the rocks. I had twisted my ankle and on the way home I was limping, screaming every now and then. Adriana had offered me her shoulder and a small stone.

"Squeeze it like that, so you'll make it pass. It's magic."

She had fished it from the water and was convinced that the shining lines in the gray matrix were gold.

"One of these days we'll come back by ourselves and get the gold from the Tavo, and then we'll be rich," she said, supporting me.

I laughed at her crazy faith, I forgot the pain in my ankle. I had kept the stone as a good-luck charm, and in the house on Via Zara I could no longer find it.

Around eight Piero returned and we sat at the kitchen table. It was still early, and too late for the two of us. Under his puffy eyes white traces of his tears remained or maybe it was the salt spray from the sea. We weren't hungry: he had a coffee and I not even that. We looked at each other fleetingly, with the timidity of people who have escaped a storm. We didn't know what wind would blow.

"What's happening to us?" I asked.

He took my hand and ran his thumb slowly over every finger, then again from the beginning.

"I'm very confused. Give me a month to figure it out," he said.

14

My mother went to bed on a Sunday, near the end of that summer. In the morning she had shelled fresh beans and kneaded flour and water for *taiaticci* without any presentiment of what would happen. At noon, a little earlier than usual, she ladled the pasta onto my father's plate and told him she wasn't well. She withdrew into the bedroom and stayed there, going only to the bathroom, supporting herself on walls and doors. She stopped eating, but every so often she drank the juice of a cold peach from the refrigerator that my father brought her. He telephoned me, after three days like that. Every so often even now he repeats that his wife cooked him his favorite pasta with her last bit of strength.

With a lot of hesitations she confessed to me that for months she had been losing "blood down below." I persuaded her to go to the hospital. The gynecologist was kind, but she emerged from his hands with her head lowered, as if violated. In fifty-six years only her husband and the town midwife had had anything to do with her intimate parts. In the hours that preceded the operation she seemed content, maybe all those doctors and nurses around gave her an unexpected sense of importance, at least there.

The head of the department took out her uterus and ovaries, the apparatus from which we six children were born.

"Have no illusions, it's already progressed," he said when they brought her back to her room, still asleep.

I remember precisely the smell of the first cup of broth that

I brought to her lips after the operation. And the slightly frightened gaze of an aged child when she leaned forward to drink. She roused in me an inextricable knot of tenderness and revulsion. I had no familiarity with her body, when they uncovered her buttocks to give her shots I wanted to go out and the nurses kept me: "You can stay, you're her daughter." Her nudity, even partial, disturbed me. I moved my eyes away from the hair on her legs. But it was my mother. It was her, my mother. She had given me to another woman to bring up, and yet I had remained her daughter. I will be forever.

The traces of Adalgisa had slowly faded from my heart. She had given me my wedding dress, she telephoned at every birthday. I seldom thought of her.

My mother occupied me inside, true and fierce. She remained in large part unknown: I never penetrated the mystery of her hidden affection. I will close my accounts with her in my last hour.

The morning cleaners turned on the light at six, and began cleaning the room. I got up from the folding chair where I had spent the night, put it back in the bathroom. I combed my mother's hair. Maybe I was looking for a nod of gratitude or at least of attention. The signs were contradictory and therefore indecipherable: for her my presence was taken for granted, a duty, but sometimes she pointed to the empty space on the greenish blanket and said rest.

My father arrived in the evening, I yielded him my place and he stood there, somewhat uncomfortable. He asked her how do you feel and she said so-so. Then they didn't know how to speak to each other, he looked with a certain fear at the familiar figure lying there—never at her face—and the drops descending slowly in the IV.

"The downstairs neighbor's jars of tomato exploded," he said after a long silence.

He had brought her some figs in a napkin.

Adriana didn't come. I hadn't seen her for a while. One afternoon she packed two bags, the last thing she did was take down the portrait of our brother, leaving an empty space on the wall.

"You're always with Vincenzo and me. Now think of your husband before someone else takes him," she said with the child in her arms.

It was the Sunday that our mother had taken to her bed, but we didn't yet know it. My sister avoided what was coming.

Piero and I met in the hospital more than at home. He talked to the doctors he knew, reassured my mother. Hearing him nearby distracted me from what we were going through. Maybe sometimes we believed we could repair the fracture and come out of it more solid and valuable, like Japanese ceramics restored with gold.

He brought my father to his office and rejuvenated him with a set of false teeth. That evening my mother, incredulous, leaned over to knock with her nail on the incisors of resin. I was almost always with her, she was so weak, my husband had all the freedom to reflect on his confusion. The time of the illness and the month he had asked for coincided.

One morning I returned to Via Zara to wash. I opened the closet, on Piero's side there were empty spaces between pants and shirts. I didn't see his sandals on the shoe rack, and his tennis clothes had also disappeared. My head was spinning, I collapsed on the bed in which he hadn't slept. The white bedspread was tight and smooth. I was losing everything: Piero, my mother, Adriana. There was something in me that summoned abandonments.

I don't know how long I stayed like that, inert. I waited that evening in the corridor of Gynecology. Women with difficult pregnancies walked by slowly in bathrobes, supported by their husbands.

"You're not sleeping at home, you're taking away your

things. Are you leaving?" I asked as soon as he came through the glass doors.

"I was in Foggia, as on every Wednesday. I stay in the hotel, you know. And I brought some things to the cleaner, end of season," he said calmly.

Piero was still protecting me with half truths, but they didn't last long. He was gripped by a secret happiness. He was waiting for my mother to die, and later I reproached him.

The doctors couldn't explain her state of weakness a week after the operation. And yet the progress was regular, the tests were normal. The liveliness of the first days had changed to torpor. Even lying down, my mother could no longer bear the struggle of living. She appended a rambling signature to a printed page and left the hospital against the advice of the doctors.

On the way home she was suddenly curious about what was passing by outside the window, then she closed her eyes for a while.

"There didn't use to be all these cars going around," she said of the traffic, shaking her head.

From the depths of an apparent sleep she asked to stop at the cemetery, she had smelled it in the air.

"Wait for me, I'll be right back," and she got out on the gravel whose pebbles she knew by heart.

I followed a short distance behind. Her son's tomb was at her height, on the wall inhabited by the dead. She didn't worry about the withered flowers in those weeks, she knew she had little time. She ran her fingers over the photograph of Vincenzo and kissed them, she steadied herself with her other hand on the stone slab that divided them. She remained like that, in a mute dialogue. It wasn't a farewell, she made an appointment for sometime soon.

She collapsed on the seat of the car, and when we got home I had to support her on the stairs. My father is wrong: she used up her last bit of strength at the cemetery.

She asked me to change the sheets for the ones from her wedding, which she had used on a single night so many years earlier. She waited, in pain, on a chair for me to find them at the back of the wardrobe. Later I understood that she had deliberately set them aside; somehow or other the thought of death had passed through her head as a girl. She returned to bed relieved. Her hands lying on the border embroidered with sprays of flowers were bones, the veins dark in relief under the transparent skin.

One by one the neighbors arrived with provisions for visiting the sick. In a few days the kitchen cabinets filled with packets of sugar, vacuum-packed coffee, crackers.

"Have something," my mother said, and I filled the moka for each of them, I served steaming cups in the bedroom while they chatted in the afternoon light.

With those who came late and some who returned a second time, she didn't even sit up against the pillows, and barely turned her head.

"I'm feeling weak," she apologized, and they talked among themselves, ate what others had brought.

She refused to return to the hospital for a checkup, and I couldn't even name the prescribed treatments.

"If the evil moment is here the illness should kill me, not the doctors," she said to the family doctor, who tried to persuade her.

Gradually she withdrew into a terminal indifference. What my mother died of I still don't know precisely. Of cancer but of much else. A sum of zeroes. Zero the value she gave to staying alive, zero her usefulness. Her children—we—were distant, in case of need we never asked her for help, advice, a glance. Her avarice had been known to us forever.

My mother devoted herself entirely to Vincenzo, in the cemetery. A kind of anesthesia protected her from us, the survivors. Like that she let Adriana escape, as one loses a coin or the house keys: as she had lost me at six months. She reserved her care for the only one who no longer needed her. How many times had I been jealous of a dead man. Memory is a form of recrimination. It's forgiveness I can't find.

In the last period she must have reviewed her scattered children. A silent appeal. Adriana reckless and nowhere to be found. Sergio in the desert drilling for oil, Domenico transplanted to the countryside. The youngest shut in to expiate a disability he would never make up for. I took care of her and my father once a week, but I was too different, the most distant of all.

It's not simple to die if the heart is strong, the lungs robust. Under the wedding sheet her body was a band of pain she couldn't abandon. Piero came with a friend who was a specialist and brought drugs to sedate her.

When my mother slept I read. In the storage area I had found some books from when I was a child. I opened one out of curiosity, out of nostalgia for Jo March who deformed the pockets of her dresses with her hands and whistled like a little boy. Without realizing it, I got to the end.

I was always in the bedroom, my father slept in the other room, in one of our beds. He took care of the shopping, proud of being able to pay immediately, ever since he had retired. He cooked the pasta and the sauce and called me when it was ready. I came out of the odor that had formed in the bedroom and couldn't eat for a moment.

One day he had finished and I was still staring at my untouched plate.

"Don't you see it's getting cold?" he burst out.

"That's my business."

"Your mamma in there can't wait for you to do as you like," he said.

I looked at him: that obtuse, egotistical man, to whom all was due. The plate of spaghetti flew past him, crashed into the wall and then onto the floor. He picked up the pieces, later.

"You go, then. Or call your sons—not one of them has showed up," I shouted.

"It's women's business, otherwise I wouldn't be here thanking a snake," he shouted, too, but a little surprised by my gesture.

"I have never heard a single thank you from your mouth."

I saw his knuckles whiten in the effort to squeeze the back of the chair. Years before he would have used his hands. But my outburst had just begun.

"I'm sick of thinking about everyone. Piero doesn't come home at night, I don't know what's going to happen to my marriage, and what do you care, you don't care anything about anyone."

"Shut up," he said softly, grinding his teeth. "Your mamma is dying."

I went back to the other room, sobbing. The truths I kept at bay had all come out together, at the wrong moment.

My mother had dirtied herself. Now I washed her in bed, using the drawsheets as I had seen the nurses do in the hospital. She slept a medicated sleep when the pain gave her some respite. At times she opened her eyes with a childlike wonder, she seemed to be present at the dawn of the world. She looked at me as if in search of explanations. I don't know if she recognized me.

My lucidity was also inconstant. I was expecting something from her, a final revelation. I imagined the words she could utter. I hoped to hear that she had loved me, but it didn't happen. Yet she didn't want anyone else around, and maybe that was a way of telling me. She was annoyed if someone entered the room. Her death absorbed us totally. We had never been so much together.

Outside of there my father went to call Domenico at the farm, and Piero tried to get in touch with Sergio in Libya. He also looked much closer to home, in Borgo Sud, asking for Adriana from house to house.

My mother died one night. The painful hunger for air of the

last hours suddenly ceased, she had no more need of it. I turned off the light and for a while remained alone to watch. The profound doubt survived of having been unworthy of her love. And, more superficially, an untamable rage. Later I called my father.

Many came to say goodbye, from the town and from the countryside; outside the house she was valued more than I would have thought. The owner of the store where I bought the dress for her insisted on adding a pin, as a gift, while Ernesto from the wine shop brought two trays of *fiadone* and *vincotto*. On the kitchen wall I had cleaned the stain from the flying spaghetti, only a trace of oil remained. My father received condolences standing up, to each he repeated, "She's not suffering anymore," indicating her face, smooth in the apparent serenity of death.

Professor Morelli arrived in the afternoon, with my colleague Michela. They asked for directions in the square and the usual group stationed in front of the café escorted them to the house. I was moved when they entered and he gave me a long embrace. I saw the checks of his jacket distorted by tears.

The most silent was Giuseppe, on a chair apart, confused by all the people. I'd gone to see him one afternoon at the institution, to prepare him. We talked on the bench at the back of the garden.

"Our mother isn't well," I had said.

"I know. I dreamed about her last night."

He went back inside to get something from his room to show me: a drawing of her hands, as they had become. One nail was blackened as if it had been crushed, or maybe it was already a sign of mourning. The fingers were joined in the exact position that they have on the breast of the dead.

Sergio returned from Libya in time to say goodbye before the coffin was closed. I didn't want to watch that moment of darkness descend on her with the lid. Only Adriana was missing.

15

I n a few steps I traverse the parking lot along the river and the death of my mother. Some cars speed along the shore, lights aimed at the asphalt. The van is hunkered in the usual place, in an indentation in the sidewalk. The night dampness obscures the windows, some dry leaves are caught under the windshield wipers. Repainted, it looks new, sticking out against the blue the red letters of a brush careful not to go outside the edges. "Taste of the Sea," it says, and beside it, smaller, on a foaming wave: "By Adriana." I clean the fogged up window and look inside. She's thrown the sweatshirt on the passenger seat, one sleeve hangs upside down to the floor. She's always hot: even in winter she's got her sleeves rolled up when she fries the fish. But now she's sleeping.

She invented this job four or five years ago. She found the van on the Tiburtina, at an auto wrecker's. I was here on vacation, she wanted me to go with her to see it before deciding.

"It's kind of banged up," I said, bewildered, walking around it.

"But it still runs, so when it's fixed up for me and painted it'll be a jewel."

I returned a few days later, with the intention of paying for it. I was too late, a friend had already taken care of it, said the demolition man. It took him a moment to remember the name Vittorio. Adriana and her desk mate hadn't completely lost sight of one another. He, too, had been living in Pescara for a while, he was designing wind parks in Abruzzo and Puglia, and they met every so often, I knew that.

For a moment I can smell fried calamari, but it must be only a trick of memory. Last July I came here, as soon as I got off the train. I didn't say anything, I got at the end of the line of customers. They come even from Montesilvano and Francavilla, Adriana is proud of that. The fishermen from Borgo bring her the baskets of fish just off the boats, that's the secret: from salt water to boiling oil, says Adriana, flouring shrimp and anchovies.

She banishes Vincenzo when he comes to help her, in the afternoons.

"Think about studying, you, you're not coming here to get smelly."

My mother asked about her, before she died.

"She's coming up," I lied.

"Have the curse removed," she said, taking a breath between the syllables.

She said nothing more after that. In the last hours I held her hand, to take her to the border. She squeezed it a moment, but maybe it was only a reflex.

I didn't understand what she meant. I was supposed to find someone who would free Adriana? The *magara* who used to be in the country had died years earlier and anyway I wouldn't have gone there. Today I say to myself that I was wrong to disregard the wish of a dying woman.

Our mother was already beside her son when Adriana entered the cemetery. A murmur of disapproval announced her, and Piero, who touched my arm. During the wake the question about her had circulated: where's the other one?

The group of neighbors parted to let her through, and she came up next to me along with a breath of wind while the town worker walled up the niche. I was absorbed by his work, by the rapid movements of his calloused hands, by the scraping of the trowel that smoothed the cement. I imagined how inside the tomb the light of day was narrowing every minute. When the brick closed up the only corner that was still open it was gone.

My sister's hair had grown back, and she held the child by the hand. With the other she sought mine and I tugged it as hard as I could. Her sunglasses fell off, exposing her, swollen and red from crying. Her nose was dripping, she couldn't find a Kleenex in her pants pockets. So I gave her one, but only to quiet the gossips. The neighbor women were pretending to read dates and names carved into the stones, but they didn't let us out of their sight. I picked up little Vincenzo, so close to the other one. He smiled at me, he was much heavier than the last time I'd seen him. It was a moment of joy. He looked in ignorance at the still unpolished tomb of his grandmother who'd hardly known him.

Sobs shook Adriana's rib cage. She was weeping with rage at the missed chance, at her superficiality. She hadn't believed in our mother's illness. The hands that had hit her were bathed in tears and mucus.

With my sister I shared a legacy of words not said, gestures omitted, care denied. And rare, unexpected kindnesses. We were daughters of no mother. We are still, as always, two girls who ran away from home.

It was the moment to say goodbye. A cloud with ragged edges covered the sun suddenly, a shudder went down my back. Relatives and neighbors filed before us with a discreet but agitated shuffling, they kissed us on the cheeks murmuring words of comfort to each, my father, my brothers, even Piero. Some skipped Adriana, seeing her in that state. Or maybe they considered her unworthy of consolation.

"You grew up in the city, but your mamma is always your mamma," a woman said to me who from the height of her balcony checked the square at all hours.

"Poor Evuccia, she never thought of herself. She sacrificed

herself for you, for the children," whispered the owner of the VéGé, who had been for years our principal and at times impatient creditor.

With her foot she bumped a vase of fake flowers, overturning it; she righted it, apologizing to the dead person it belonged to.

There was also Odilia, who had come in the Ape, bringing in the back the dog, now old, and three sheep, who knows why. She had parked at the end of the avenue. She and Adriana didn't even look at each other. Last, a man from a distant district approached, whose hair smelled of stables.

"The woman was a saint, now she's in the world of truth. Bear up, friends, bear up," he repeated, disconsolate.

He insisted on leaving me a bag of fresh eggs wrapped in newspaper, I was to beat one every morning with sugar and marsala, for breakfast. With that I would regain my strength, he said in the wind that bent the cypresses.

I found nothing to say, only some brief nods of assent. My mother described by others was not the same I knew.

Vincenzo rested his head in the hollow of my neck, a warm secure place. They all looked at him with half smiles of politeness or pity, for his birth, which no one had heard about, for the father who wasn't to be seen.

We turned our backs on the tombs and headed toward the gate. My mother remained behind the bricks and the still damp mortar. Someone from the town asked Sergio how life was in Libya.

Lightning struck very close, in front of us. The jagged line of light and a kind of click, the votive lamps went out and there was a crash of thunder. The rain, so violent, was only the beginning. There was barely time for everyone to squeeze into the little portico when hail arrived. The greenish sky unloaded balls of ice, not pebbles. They cut down the alfalfa in a field, the branches of trees, a garden in the distance. Behind us the hail fell indifferently on the tombs: marble and granite, photographs of the dead, celebratory phrases in letters of gold or silver. Only a few severed stalks of chrysanthemums and daisies remained.

Odilia's dog came first, running madly along the avenue under that hail of frozen bullets. The sheep, too, jumped out of the back of the Ape and followed him. They sheltered in the portico in search of their mistress, stuck their noses among the crowded bodies, asking for protection. One trembled with cold and fright on unsteady legs, its nostrils dilating as it breathed. The strong odor of wet wool mingled with the ozone of the lightning.

I was shivering in a shirt that was too summery, Piero put his jacket over my shoulders. It had a new smell. Adriana was no longer weeping, and had taken Vincenzo back.

We looked at each other: not even the bass drum of the band had ever produced the din that our mother drew down from the sky at her funeral.

The hail stopped as suddenly as it had started. Rivulets of water tinged with earth ran everywhere, but the thunder was now a distant rumble. I returned to the city with Piero, keeping his jacket on. It seemed to me that I was leaving the town forever. I would visit my father countless times, but it wouldn't be as before. Steam rose from the wet countryside, water was still streaming down the embankments. Toads crossed the road with their prehistoric gait and an incomprehensible urgency. Many ended up crushed by the tires of cars, they were yellow, belly up, feet fixed in the air. In the rearview mirror I saw the place where my mother had lived and I had been her daughter disappear.

I had lost Adriana and Vincenzo at a certain point. I had lost them under the portico, amid thunder and people, the backs of the sheep and our silent farewell to the girls we were no longer. Certainly she hadn't gone by the house later, either.

She returned to Pescara with someone, she drove the same curves, a few kilometers ahead or behind. And while we were gone, the neighbors in our dining room uncovered the trays of cold food they had prepared, they twisted off the bottle tops and offered the carbonated drinks to those present. They consumed the funeral banquet in honor of "that dearly departed."

I had lost her again, but I wasn't worried. Adriana knew where to find me.

We drove without speaking, Piero concentrated on the road. Every so often he swerved to avoid a toad. Sometimes I looked at his perfect and impenetrable profile that shifted as the car hit a pothole or a bump in the asphalt lifted by the roots of the pines. Once he took his hand off the gear shift and took mine that lay abandoned in my lap. He squeezed it and warmed it until he had to change gears.

In Via Zara he stopped in front of the entrance. I ignored the mailbox overflowing with envelopes and went up while he parked. I hadn't been home for days, the apartment smelled musty, of two different absences. I opened some windows. On the balcony the hortensias had died of thirst.

I waited for him, sitting at the kitchen table, with the light on. The days were getting shorter, the dark and threatening edge of the storm that had burst inland filled the sky.

He rang the bell, as if the house were no longer his.

"Your keys?" I asked him.

"I can't find them, I must have forgotten them in the office," he said.

He had gone to get milk at the store at the corner of Viale Kennedy—that had delayed him. He poured it in the milk pan to warm, while he took out our twin cups, the biscuits. He didn't remember where the sugar was. He also sat down, we ate awkwardly in the white light that was too strong. It was our last dinner in that kitchen, with milk and slightly stale biscuits.

Even now, as I'm returning to the hotel near Via Zara, I

don't know if he really intended to stay there that night. He got up to wash the cups and I went to bed. He must have heard the sobs as he passed the closed door of the dark room. It was my turn to cry. He came in and sat beside me, held me tight, for a long time. Sometimes he trembled slightly. He dried my tears with his thumbs and kissed my salty eyes, nose, mouth. I was weeping for all my losses, past and present, including him. He comforted me and he was the same who was leaving me, we both knew it.

A muffled cry when I bit his lip, then we kissed more deeply. He undressed furiously and was already between the sheets. I didn't move, unsure whether to welcome him.

"You don't want to?" he asked in the low voice of recovered desire.

I didn't answer, I turned my back. He talked to my favorite vertebra, he nibbled it a little. He thrust and withdrew, his sex increasingly hard. I had his hand on my stomach, I gave in. He slid inside me.

That, too, was the last time.

16.

I slept as I hadn't for a long while. I woke suddenly, and it took me a few moments to recognize the room, already light, and Piero lying on his side. My mother had been buried for some hours and I was no longer in the town.

He looked at me when I opened my eyes. He seemed thinner, a new tic agitated one eyelid. The summer tan had faded, leaving on his cheeks two small vertical, symmetrical wrinkles, his nose slightly peeling. I reached out my hand toward him, and he stiffened. He seemed a different person from the night before.

"What's wrong?" I asked.

Basically I hoped he would continue to be silent. We would stay together in the bad feeling that at that moment was spreading in waves from his half of the bed. Maybe it would pass, one day, without a reason, the way it had come.

Piero gave himself only the time for a few breaths, I think, or it was a longer pause. He was twisting the edge of the sheet in his fingers.

"I've wanted to tell you for a long time. But don't look at me."

So I turned toward the wall outfitted as a closet. Some fragments are missing in the memory of that morning, the moment Piero began remains confused, no matter how great an effort I make to find it again.

"Last winter I met a person."

He spoke in short sentences, every word fell on the bed clear and straight as a knife.

"Afterward I swore to you that it wouldn't happen again. One night, while you were sleeping."

He recounted to my back the silent struggle against a strong and urgent call. At times his voice broke, I waited motionless for him to resume.

"I tried to resist, suffocating my desires. But I felt dead."

I listened to him in the light that pervaded the room, entering through the sliding door, which was open. At times he was sure that I had understood, he said, but everything went on as before.

"In April there was another chance encounter, then I stopped counting."

The bags and suitcases arranged on a high shelf had descended to the floor. We didn't travel often, but he continued over the years to buy different shapes and sizes. Some, never used, still had the labels with the brands and those small locks. Suddenly they were there down below, ready to leave. And above hung the empty hangers of Piero's shirts and jackets. They left exposed the dress I had worn to his graduation party in the country, with the halo of blood still on the chest. I had kept it as a souvenir. The stain brought back pieces of that day. The long kiss at the table, amid the applause of the guests.

"I'm tired of lying to you," Piero said.

His mother, who was secretly handing him something and spoke to him in a whisper. I had turned for a moment toward Adriana and had found on the plate the velvet case. It contained a ring of white gold and diamonds, the right size for my left ring finger. Costanza was moved, she had chosen it. The celebration intensified.

"I didn't want to make you suffer," Piero repeated, out of synch.

My mother had said this would happen, and the drainpipe had fallen, too. Blood had dripped from my cheekbone onto the dress. While lunch resumed inside, Adriana and I had tried to clean it, but the fibers of the fabric were saturated. The mark had to remain, obstinate and fierce, incomprehensible.

How many other signs had I neglected? Who was my husband? The betrayal he was confessing became almost secondary. I didn't understand in what corner of himself he had hidden the suffering that was pouring out of his mouth all at once.

I struggled to keep myself whole, solid on the bed. Piero sat up, stared at a precise point in space. I also sat up, listening to what was still to come. His story shifted back in time, to July two years earlier. He had discovered the Baia del Cecetto, in Vasto, and there had been various occasional encounters there, but without consequences. Also in the dunes of Tollo, just sex. He used the same word, continuously, encounters. Every time it was a wound driven deeper into my flesh.

He was always going to the beach in that period, his father took care of the office move. I was in Chieti at the time, examining students in hot classrooms and passing notes to Professor Morelli with the proposed grade, which he would confirm or not. In the majority of cases he raised the twenty-eight to thirty, while my husband was meeting lovers in Cecetto or in the dunes.

I didn't think of that while Piero was talking. I was cold, my back leaning against the headboard. The same shivers I had the day we had become engaged. I'm always cold when something powerful happens to me.

Costanza had taken me to her room to look for a sweater. Here, green and soft, with her perfume at the neck and wrists. I had put it on and the blood on the dress was covered up. I thought of that, of the color of Costanza's sweater that was perhaps a petroleum green—I have a partial blindness for the chromatic shades. And of her, who was organizing the wedding.

"It will be beautiful. It's magnificent that Piero has found a girl like you."

"And your husband is pleased?" I asked doubtful.

I was afraid that Dr. Rosati aspired to a wife who had grown up in the cream of Pescarese society for his only son.

"Nino is a reserved man, but I assure you that he is extremely pleased."

When she was happy Costanza talked in superlatives.

"You are precious for Piero. We couldn't wish anything better for him."

He seemed calmer now, sitting beside me. Gradually, as he emptied himself out, he managed also to look at me every so often. Only his eyelid beat madly.

"In the fall I continued to see the same people, more or less. I saw them in some bars here in Pescara, or outside the center."

He listed them: Heroes, Rainbow Club, the sauna at Silvi Marina. I who thought I knew the city and its outskirts had never heard of them. For me they were always dinners with friends from climbing.

In the afternoon the sky had cleared, the air was warm again. The guests had said goodbye, they left with the tulle-wrapped red favors. Piero and I had gone out on the grass that was already dry. He had caressed me with his index finger around the new wound before examining the gutter lying on the ground.

"It broke because of a little rain," he had said, touching it with one foot.

I also thought of that strange accident.

After the celebration we had rushed toward marriage, without understanding what was happening. Not that we minded. We were in love, or at least the need for something to which I could give his name and he mine united us. We would have a place for us alone.

Piero's mother, tireless, thought of everything. One day we asked her, why such a hurry.

"If you don't hurry it'll end," she said in a low voice.

She looked at us, now one, now the other, with apprehensive eyes.

She had found the apartment in Via Zara, an opportunity not to miss, with that view of the sea, she repeated. Her husband tore off the checks: one for the deposit, the more substantial at the moment of purchase. We had chosen the architect, and with a few touches and a clever repartitioning of the rooms the house had become functional. Like our marriage, at the beginning.

"My parents were always ashamed of me, for some reason or another, one year because I'd been failed, another because of the earring. When you arrived, they had you to be proud of," Piero said.

I don't know how his parents had entered into the flow of words, at times I lost the thread of the truth he was revealing. He rested one hand on the blanket where my leg was, I barely felt the pressure. I don't know if he was trying to console me or still holding on to me. I grabbed his ring finger which was missing the ring and began to twist it backward, toward the arm. He didn't react. He spoke freely, after all that silence. He seemed lighter beside me, liberated. I sank under the weight that he had supported for so long. He was passing it on to me.

I didn't even want to imagine him as he furtively entered a night club, much less coming out, with his hair mussed, the stench of the close air and smoke, of alcohol and sex. How many times had I heard him from the bed lingering in the shower after those invented dinners. Then he came into the bedroom fragrant with our bath foam.

I didn't recognize him in his story, I didn't recognize the man who had come with me to Gagliardi for the wedding registry. We had had fun. Formal set of china, informal set for evenings with friends. Some silly things we couldn't give up, said the saleswoman: two vases from Venini, the orange squeezer in the shape of a spider. She was devouring Piero with greedy looks. In those months I felt so honored to enter the Rosati family.

The day of the wedding the whole town was in the square. When I passed by on the arm of my father, so stiff, those who were behind stood up on tiptoe to see the bride. And they didn't want to miss the arrival of the people from Pescara, in their shiny cars, the elegant women who got out holding up the edge of their dresses.

Adriana followed me, spreading over the cobblestones the long train I'd wanted. The high-heeled shoes were tight, every so often she yelled ow! and cursed, her voice a little too loud. She was my witness, dressed in red and with the usual bold expression. The townspeople whispered behind her back; Piero's relatives were crazy about her.

"A pleasure," she introduced herself, "I'm the bride's witness and also her sister."

My mother was a little emotional in a blue suit with large cream-colored flowers, maybe that day she had changed her ideas about my marriage: maybe it would succeed.

The boy who had carried the box with the rings to the altar had had fun knotting the ribbon around it. Undoing it had taken some time, with Adriana's frantic fingernails. The priest had joked about the knots of love and again I hadn't picked up the sign. We had exchanged rings and kissed, we had believed in all the promises recited by heart.

"The first time it happened on the beach, there was a wind," Piero said.

He was returning to the summer of two years before, he was going into details. I wasn't sure I wanted to support his need to confess everything, but I didn't stop him. I continued to force his finger and he didn't resist.

"You know there are nude beaches in Abruzzo?"

As girls Adriana and I had gone to one of those places by mistake. I must have been seventeen and she three years younger, it was the period of our hitchhiking adventures. My sister had glanced around, without even putting down her straw bag.

"Look, it's full of dirty old men, let's get out of here," she'd said.

I lacked the will to tell Piero, I shook my head no and he continued. I stared at the dress on the hanger, it seemed to me that it was oscillating slightly. It was an optical illusion, the air in the room remained motionless, there was no earthquake. It was me falling.

"At first I looked and that was all—there were people sunbathing and couples who withdrew."

I pushed sharply and something in his hand yielded. A cry escaped him and I let go, on the blanket the ring finger was already swelling and darkening. I didn't believe I had used so much force. I was bathed in tears, I had no idea when I'd started crying.

That morning the bay was almost deserted, the clouds were running swiftly. He was lying naked on the towel, at every gust the sand like a thousand pinpricks hit his back. He had fallen asleep.

"You're burning here where you're white," the voice had said and a hand ran over his buttocks.

He had let him do that for some moments, then he turned over, revealing his erection. He had seen the smile in the dazzling light of midday. The other had knelt on the ripples shaped by the wind, had begun to lick and suck it.

"It happened completely naturally," my husband said. "You're the only one I can talk to about it."

He didn't even know the name of that boy and had never met him again. Maybe he was there on vacation or maybe only for him, to let him know what he really wanted.

17

He had stayed there unmoving, the sun dried the sweat and a man's saliva. Nerves and muscles exhausted by pleasure, he had been unable to say anything to him. Eyes closed, he had heard him get up, and then his feet light on the sand. He left like that, like someone who had delivered a gift.

Later an unexpected anguish had awakened him. The wind had fallen, the sky was cloudy over the rough sea. His skin was burning, he ran to the shore. From there he had turned to look back, the orange terrycloth towel with the imprint of his body. He had gone swimming in the solitude of the bay, swimming furiously as if he had to reach the Tremiti islands.

He had arrived home soon after I did. A long shower and he had helped me make dinner with his usual gentleness, or even more. At night he groaned in bed, maybe because of his dreams or the burn I hadn't seen.

He imposed on himself a discipline in his thoughts, in his behavior. Not to desire men, instantly turn your eyes away from someone you like. Careful with those who look at you insistently, who have recognized you. Avoid fantasies about men when you're with your wife. You're happy, this desire is not useful. You've always kept it at bay, and it will disappear, sooner or later.

Piero controlled himself, for a while. One day his secretary telephoned, the doctor hadn't come back from lunch and the patient was getting agitated in the waiting room. He wasn't at home with me, at that moment he was in a public toilet, he who was so obsessed with hygiene. It was empty, but right away a man around forty arrived. Among all the urinals available he chose the one next to his and began touching himself, looking at it, panting. Piero leaned one hand on the wall and with the other masturbated rapidly, his head now turned to the neighbor, now to the door. They came together, each in his own urinal. A few minutes later he apologized to the patient—a long line in the bank, he put on smock and gloves. He asked the assistant to prepare the cement for the permanent crowns.

The dike he had held up for so many years had now been knocked down. A new life began, of lies, fear of discovery, stolen pleasures. Piero was born a second time.

But he was restless, he was never in the right place. Not with me: his desire drew him elsewhere. Not in the places where the encounters happened, inhabited by guilt. An autumn of bad weather had arrived, and the beaches more to the south weren't practical. The meeting place in San Luigi seemed to him dangerous, he felt too exposed outside, after all Pescara wasn't such a big city. Gossip flew from one end to the other and his was a prominent family. His father and mother and their bourgeois circle frightened him much more than me. He recalled Costanza—always composed, impeccable—imitating when he was a boy the slightly waggling gait of a neighbor, and his shrill voice. She laughed at the man, slapping her thigh. Piero would never have wanted his parents to know, he was afraid of knowing it himself. He was the first to be mistaken.

In the dark rooms of the clubs that he had started going to he felt more protected, but the smallest thing alarmed him. What if some patient had seen him? Even in the dim light he had picked out, in the naked forms of one body rubbing against another, Maurizio, a high-school classmate. During a school trip he had pushed him against a parked bus, trying to kiss him on the mouth. Piero had fled, then, disturbed more than anything by the revolution that was bursting in his pants. He had no idea if Maurizio, called Zizzi, had recognized him in the instantaneous moment of a glance.

Then he met a man from Bari who lived by himself in an apartment near the stadium, and he went every so often to see him there. Bed, couch, two in the shower, no hiding. But also pasta eaten together in front of the television, white wine from the fridge, clinking glasses. The other asked him to stay overnight and one night he agreed, in the weakness after orgasm. He came home in the morning, with the apologies and lies ready for me. Some nights the certainty of being thrown out of the house woke him. The suitcases he had bought awaited him, new, in the dressing room.

His lover began to claim more, wanted him all for himself.

"You know I can't," said Piero.

The Barese complained in his melodic cadence, became annoying. The relationship with a married man, which at first he had found so exciting, now bothered him.

"I'm going to speak to your wife," he threatened once.

"I won't leave her for you," Piero told him, picking up his jacket.

He never went back. He was afraid only that the man might really look for me. But he had never given him his number, not even his last name. The only trace that remained of him in the apartment in the stadium neighborhood was a name thought of with a Barese accent, with nostalgia.

For days, weeks, or perhaps months Piero deluded himself that desire was sated. The sex of the last period had been enough, this he believed. He could return with all of himself to our life of two, which was so pleasant, and without risks. He was very affectionate with me, he planned exotic vacations, a trip to Mexico. He mentioned a baby, a boy, or, rather, a girl, he went so far as to imagine her look, her similarities.

"We'll name her Alessia, or Viola," he imagined.

And at night, when I reached from the bed to take the pill: "Isn't it time to stop it?"

He sought me. The novelty was that he asked me to suck his nipples, first. He penetrated me from behind, holding me tight, kissing my neck, my shoulders. But then sometimes he got lost inside me, his penis became small and soft, slid out. I didn't care, only the flesh remained unsatisfied, in its slightly painful tension. We remained in an embrace like two comrades in the black night.

Certainly he wasn't thinking of breaking his abstinence when he accepted an invitation to a birthday party in one of those clubs. He told me that he was going, but he spoke of a new restaurant near the port. Maybe he felt so secure that he could test himself, maybe he really thought that desire was spent.

At first he liked nothing about the evening, he wanted to leave quickly. The decorations were overdone, the music too loud, the festoons with miniature phalluses were ridiculous. The men were bare-chested, shiny with oils, many already in underpants. Suddenly a young man jumped onto a table and started dancing. Unlike the others he was wearing tight jeans and a white undershirt, the strobe lamp illuminated him. Piero was attracted by the strong, primitive feet that beat on the wood, the almost prehensile toes. He didn't come from a dancing school, but he was enchanting. Everyone stopped to watch him, and at the end some of the more pumped up fought with obscene cries over the soaking wet undershirt he had thrown to the crowd. He jumped down and came over to Piero, drying himself with a bandanna. They had a mojito and talked at the bar. Then they withdrew to a corner sheltered from the noise, the lights. They undid each other's pants, began to touch each other.

"Dr. Rosati . . ." the youth whispered in Piero's ear.

"What do you know about what my name is?"

"Pescara isn't Los Angeles. We saw each other a few years ago, you don't remember? You came to the celebration in Borgo Sud, we danced in the square till late. Later I met you a few times at Centrale," he said, trying to turn him toward the wall.

Piero escaped, composed himself in a hurry.

"You're taking me for someone else."

His hand trembled as he zipped the zipper, and it got stuck halfway.

"I have to go," he said.

"Bye, doctor," the sailor said, disappointed.

What Piero most feared had happened: he had been recognized. In the car he punched the steering wheel, cursed. We hadn't seen Adriana for a while, but surely she was around Borgo and the sailor knew her. He might tell her about that encounter, she would tell me. He wept as he drove home, and bought all the roses from a peddler who was coming out of Ferraioli disappointed. He wanted to give them to me, before I left him.

He dropped them on me, already in bed, and hurried to the bathroom. When he came back to the room I asked him to put the flowers in a vase and if he was crazy. But really he had only had a nice thought, and I regretted my rudeness.

"Give me a Tavor tablet," he said darkly.

For a while he deserted the mountains and his only outlet was tennis. He worked with his father and went out only with me, for the shopping or to the movies. We saw all the episodes of *Heimat 2* at the Sant'Andrea, Morelli had suggested it and Piero was also a fan. He became friendly with the cinema-loving Pescaresi who at first had seemed boring to him. Sometimes we'd walk along the river, he'd always be looking down, observing the dogs on their leashes.

He came home from the office with an anxiety I couldn't explain. He calmed down when he understood from my tone of voice that no one had told me anything and our marriage had survived another day. We took Tavor every night.

Then it happened. It must have been a moment of weakness, the other caught him off guard. They'd known each other by sight for years, they'd gone to the same school, the same beach club. There was no reason to fear him, Piero didn't avert his eyes in time.

It was a matter merely of organizing a tennis tournament for members of the club, for that they stayed on after the match. Or they arrived together at Dolci Sport to choose the right shoes for red clay or some cartons of balls. They decided whether to get white or yellow, more visible in the artificial light. It was for the pleasure of being together that they talked at length about the grip of a sole as if there were no problem more important. Sometimes they lingered over an aperitivo and then Piero returned home with an adolescent restlessness, an accumulated energy. He startled at the least thing, charged as he was.

Davide Ricci won the tournament. He drove my husband home after the final dinner, pulled the car over in a dark section of Via Zara. They kissed suddenly in the front seat of the Golf, with a hunger in their mouths, just down the street from No. 20 and me, at risk of being seen by someone in the building. By now it didn't matter to them.

An hour or two must have passed: it was that night, while I slept, that Piero swore to me not to see him again. They were already in love; Davide wasn't like the others. My husband's resistance lasted only a few months, he waited for spring to surrender.

In May they were in the stands at the Foro Italico for the tennis Internationals, Davide had insisted. I knew about an intensive course in implants in Rome, an entire week. It was their honeymoon. Jim Courier won that year.

18

The day begins and I'm almost in front of the hotel. On the other side of the street the sea is exposed, the lifeless beach of in-between seasons. I never walk so early, my leg muscles are warm and my stomach empty. A car parked next to the sidewalk, Piero asleep with his head against the window. He's an hour early for our meeting, and who knows how long he's been here. I've never seen him in this car. His mouth is slightly open, a small area of the glass fogs up when he exhales. Fifteen times a minute, he told me, but maybe it's twelve or even less during the sleep of an athlete. The vertical wrinkle has become a furrow on his cheek. And he has more white hair, of course.

I knock softly with my knuckles and smile. He opens his eyes suddenly, returns the smile. We stay a few moments like that, without moving. I've never been completely cured of him, something still contracts inside me. The sensation of a dip or a bump, a schoolmate of mine who fell in love easily used to call it. But now it's light, tamed, only an attenuated reflex that hasn't completely disappeared over the years.

He turns the key and presses the button on the window. Hi, he says, instinctively running his hand through the hair crushed by the window.

We go into the hotel. The dining room is empty, the tables waiting for the guests to awaken, on each a white sugar bowl. The girl who brought me the milk in my room brings *ciambellone* and *cornetti* from the kitchen.

We sit near the window, with a view of the sea, as when we were a couple on vacation. But we aren't, and suddenly I wonder what I'm doing here with him, while nearby the irreparable might happen. A man, freshly shaved, comes down, greets us with a nod. Every so often he looks at us as he's leafing through the paper, I don't know who we are to his eyes. Neither spouses nor lovers, I would tell him, never enemies.

I can't even eat the end I've torn off the *cornetto*, I just break it in pieces.

"At least put more sugar in the cappuccino," Piero insists.

I drink a little, ask how he is. He's well, going less frequently to the mountains, and he's given up scaling the north face of the Camicia. He doesn't regret his father's office, Vertigo keeps him very busy and its members are increasing. Maybe I look bewildered, and he reminds me what he's talking about: his rock-climbing gym, the first in Pescara. He has no reason to worry about my memory, it's only that I'm swallowed up in this wait. And for years I've forgotten the details of his life after me.

And me? I shrug: I oversee the students' dissertations and the Italian-language courses. I'm organizing a conference, but now I'll have to put it off.

He smiles and shakes his head. Maybe he wanted to know more, if I'm seeing someone, for example. I could tell him about my friends, about the man I saw last fall, about Christophe and our cat. My voice fails. Tactfully he doesn't mention his companion.

After breakfast we have before us all the time to fill until noon. Piero suggests a drive.

"Let's go to Borgo Sud," I say.

He drives with concentration, his profile against the light of day a drawing I always carry with me.

He slows at the first buildings, some men are working on

the side of the street with a pneumatic drill. A woman drags a drooping shopping cart, the wheels joggle on the bumpy asphalt. We cross the square with the wooden boat in the middle. I indicate the direction to Piero with my hand.

"You're sure? He'll be there?" he asks.

I'm sure only of passing by. The doors and windows of the green house are closed, the only sign of recent life is a pile of empty crates in front, the kind that hold fish. Some have fallen down, some skinny kittens are playing in them, look-alikes, with their fur sticking up. We're stopped, the engine off.

"You want to get out?" Piero asks me.

"Let's go," I say abruptly. "Take me to the hospital, I'll wait there."

They'll let us in soon.

"I phoned the doctor on call. Condition is serious but stable," he answered my first question this morning.

Besides, he has nothing new to report. No one knows exactly what happened.

I can't bear the way we're just wasting time, him talking to me about other things. I repeat, leave me at the entrance, but he won't hear of it. He parks and goes with me.

On the floor stripes of different colors guide one toward the different departments, the names are written above: red leads to Nuclear Medicine, blue to Hematology, yellow Intensive Care. At the intersections of the corridors some of the stripes turn, we follow the yellow.

A woman comes toward me with arms wide, an excited smile. She hugs me, she has a sweetish perfume, of the sort she liked even back then. She steps away and we look at each other after all these years: Gabriella, high-school classmate. She tells me in a burst her life, job at the post office, three children, one in London. I'm in a hurry, I have no desire to listen to her. Now she'll ask about me, already she's looking at Piero. He introduces himself only by name.

"What are you doing here?" Gabriella asks.

"I'm going to see someone."

At the intercom we're told that it's too early for visits, but we can sit in the waiting room and take a number. It's No. 1, at least we'll be first to talk to the doctors and go into the ward. We're in a half basement, the light filtering down from the windows mingles with the fluorescence. We stand in the middle of the room, on the walls are two large posters showing our mountains, Little Tibet with the snowdrops flowering. Underneath is a plaque with the name of the giver. I read some phrases engraved in silver or written on framed papers. A boy recounts a terrible accident and the darkness he would not have returned from without the treatment received here. They are the survivors, it's their gratitude to the doctors and nurses, to God. The dead have written nothing.

Someone rings the bell, I don't know why I go toward the door. After a few moments it rings again and someone knocks lightly with his knuckles. I look at Piero and don't dare to open. Finally an automatic control unlocks it from somewhere or other. My father enters.

"You, too?" he asks.

His mouth trembles convulsively and his voice is unsteady. His eyes redden immediately but they stay dry. My father doesn't cry. He opens his arms and beats his angry hands against his legs, the one with the two missing fingers makes a different sound. I got here last night on the train, I say, drying myself with a Kleenex.

He came from the town. I don't find him so shabby, he's straightened his hair with a wet comb, as is customary. He's wearing a dark jacket with a bit of dandruff on the shoulders, his pants are clean and pressed.

Ginetta, the widow on the ground floor, helps him with the laundry. Underwear and socks he washes himself in the sink, out of modesty. On Monday Adriana goes and airs out the rooms, cleans and straightens. They reconciled, after the death of our mother. Without saying anything she started going there one day a week and without saying anything he welcomed her, or at least didn't throw her out. Sometimes my sister brings fresh fish and cooks it: he's always a little reluctant, he's not used to it. He likes fried anchovies, which he eats with all the bones, but he eats only the tentacles of the calamari, and they have to be crunchy. This Adriana told me, shaking her head. But she is no good at ironing, especially the crease in the pants: it's always crooked. So Ginetta takes care of that. In exchange my father drives her to do the heavier shopping and in the fall piles up wood for her in the garage.

Piero approaches and holds out his hand; he ignores it. He responds with a nod, I don't understand if it's a contemptuous greeting or a silent question: what are you doing here. He sits with his chest leaning forward, elbows on his knees. Every so often he holds his head for a moment, compresses the despair inside. He doesn't have words to express it, if he released it there would be shouts, curses, as when Vincenzo died.

I also sit down, not right next to him, I leave an empty seat between us. Piero has retreated to the opposite side of the waiting room; the time doesn't pass. My father looks straight ahead, sometimes he remembers me and turns for a moment with those eyes.

The bell rings again, the door opens right away. A group of people enter talking agitatedly, crying. A relative of theirs has just been admitted. A woman supported by a man who is also in shock, they must be the parents. Two girls sobbing together, this we don't know how to do. The contrast of their smooth hair as they embrace, dyed black and blond. One is the girl-friend and the other the sister of the boy in intensive care, from what they're saying. It was an accident on the job, he was crushed by a forklift.

It's almost noon, I say to my father, so we'll have information from the doctors soon and then they'll let us go into the ward, one at a time.

"He doesn't have anything to do with our family anymore," and he points to Piero with his chin.

The other relatives arrive all together exactly at noon, they take a number and wash their hands. They sit in an orderly way, now they know one another and some exchange news on their families. Others remain silent and closed.

No. 1 in the doctors' room, a nurse comes to say, pointing to a door. I'm almost inside, with my heart racing and my stomach tight in a spasm. I turn and there's only Piero, my father stayed there.

"Papa, come."

He signals no with his head and I don't have time to persuade him.

A table separates us from the doctor, and on it is the folder with the name. The doctor opens it but almost never consults it, he has everything in his mind. He is professional, friendly. He talks to me and occasionally looks at Piero. They met yesterday.

"It's a trauma from the fall. The neurosurgeon drained the subdural hematoma and at present the vital parameters are stable, she has a strong constitution. Soon you can see her, don't be shocked."

I ask if there will be permanent damage. He pauses briefly.

"Now we're working to keep her alive, every other assessment is premature. She's sedated, in a few days we'll decrease the drugs and we'll see," he says.

I had other questions for him, but I don't remember them. Piero takes me back to the waiting room.

I search for words for my father, but he knows. He came yesterday. He doesn't talk to the doctors, nor does he go in to see Adriana. He waits for a nurse from the town to come out of the ward for a moment to tell him something he can understand. While I was talking to the doctor, she called him aside and translated the same news.

"No. 1 can dress," says a young voice. I go into a sort of corridor with some lockers, hands deliver to me what's needed: gloves, mask, single-use booties. The same hands help me lace behind my neck and back the green surgical smock that's too big for me. It's happening very fast now. I returned from Grenoble for this and I'm not ready. I hesitate, after putting on what I have to.

"Come," and the usual palm accompanies me with a light pressure on the shoulder. Along the corridor, then we turn, another corridor with white lights that are too bright. I hear our muffled footsteps on the linoleum, why so fast? We arrive in intensive care.

19.

She's pale as she never has been: she likes to appear tan even in winter. At the least warmth she's exposed, to attract every ray of sun. Now what remains of the tan is a yellowish color on her bare arms, where there are no bruises. There's a tube in her mouth, the part that's outside is corrugated. Her oxygen goes through it.

She's never that still when she sleeps, she turns and tosses, drags the sheets, kicks a foot out. Now in this artificial sleep she's motionless; occasionally the eyes roll upward in the crack between the eyelids, and remain fixed on the white. A large bruise disfigures half her forehead and face, shading from blue to purple. They cut some of her hair on that side, before the operation. I remember when Rafael's creditors butchered it, in Borgo Sud. Here they've tied the hair that's left in a side ponytail, with an elastic net bandage. They must also have taken off her makeup, I can just see some traces of the black pencil she uses lavishly.

I can't believe she's lying in this bed, with her back elevated. It all seems a mistake, an exchange of people. I struggle to recognize in the swollen face some features that resemble her. Someone will come soon and say it's not Adriana or I'm not her sister. I must have dreamed the phone call, the train journey, and that I am here.

I clutch the edge of the bed, to keep at least me in the world, to resist the lightness that invades me, coming up from my feet. As for her, I'm afraid to touch her, to hurt her. The sheet covers her fractures, one is in a cast. The nurse's gaze watches over me, attentive to my reactions. "Lori" is written on her uniform.

"You can touch her," she says.

I run my palm over her inert hand, just long enough to feel the warmth through the glove, and an alarm sounds, like a bell, *ding ding ding*. I pull back, scared.

"Don't worry, the oximeter is very sensitive to movements," the woman reassures me and stops it.

"What is it?" I ask.

"It measures the concentration of oxygen in the blood," and she points to one of the waves on the monitor.

I can touch Adriana again, but this time I choose her arm. It's soft, alive. It has a medicinal smell. I get close to her ear, I call her in a low voice.

"I'm here, don't worry if you can't respond right now."

I intercept Lori's eyes, bordered by the thick frames of her glasses.

"Does she hear me?" I ask.

"Talk to her, it's important."

A thread of saliva drips from her half-open mouth, the nurse dries it with some gauze. Adriana would be ashamed, but she doesn't know it.

"I brought you the candies you like from Grenoble, the salted butter caramels," I say stupidly.

The last time she ate them all, one by one, like a greedy child. If she were awake now she would make fun of me, imitating my pronunciation of "Grenoble" with the silent "e," the exaggerated "r." I caress her cheek with the back of my index finger. On the other she has some stitches.

I try to restrain my tears, then I realize that Adriana can't see this, either, can't hear it. I let them flow. My nose starts dripping and I don't have my purse, or Kleenex in my pocket. I dry my face with the sleeve of the smock.

They found her on the pavement behind the building where she lives with Vincenzo, at nine in the morning, two days ago. An anonymous caller had dialed 118. The ambulance got there in a few minutes, shrill notes of the siren on the bridge and then in the streets of Borgo Sud. When the crew got out there was no one with her, a woman unconscious on the ground. She was wearing a yellow dress, one shoe upside down beside the discomposed body. The other remained on the building's communal terrace, where she was when she fell. On the second floor she hit an awning, perhaps her salvation. I no longer remember where Piero heard the news, from the 118 doctor, but also from the police, I think.

She was hanging out the laundry. After breakfast Vincenzo goes to school and she usually gets ready to go out, at the last minute she goes up with the basket of clothes just out of the washing machine. She leaves them in the sea breeze, while she goes to do the shopping and other errands, sometimes stopping for a coffee in the center. Carefully dressed and made up, she sits at a table outside, looks at the people passing by. I can't imagine it, how she could have fallen from up there. Certainly she didn't want to.

On the terrace they found Vincenzo's sheets already hanging on the line with the clothespins, but the pillowcase and the tablecloth were still wet in the blue basket. The fall interrupted the work of this hand that I'm now holding in mine, careful not to alarm the oximeter again.

"What do you think, that she jumped?" I almost shouted at Piero before arriving at the hospital.

I couldn't bear any longer his way of saying the word "accident" with a hesitation, a shadow of doubt in his voice.

"The police have to consider it, as a hypothesis."

"The police don't know her, you do," and I turned toward the window.

I have no idea what happened to her yellow dress. The

emergency crew must have cut it, she'll be angry about that. I promise I'll get her a more elegant one, we'll go and choose it together at Santomo.

Here she's naked under the sheet, I glimpse the electrodes attached to her chest. A catheter carries the urine to a transparent bag hanging from the bed, there's blood in it. Her body is a battlefield, every orifice occupied. She's unarmed, others fight for her. She puts into it her obstinate beating heart, a will that's sleeping but alive.

She has already escaped more than once. She was saved from a dog bite (a scar furrows one shin), from a car with defective brakes that missed her by a few centimeters, a high fever with measles. I've always thought she was invincible, I will not see her death.

My sister is rash, she doesn't calculate limits, she's one with the world. She is prudent only where her son is concerned. This morning Piero and I went by her house. There was a trace of blood, swept up with the sawdust. A little distance away a napkin stuck on a stem of dry grass. Maybe it had blown away and she fell trying to catch it, or a clothespin, or only one of her crazy thoughts. It's an instant: an illusion of omnipotence seizes us, in the next it has betrayed us.

She'll save herself now, too, only she's taking some time. The first forty-eight hours have passed.

But I'm scared. Under those lights she's so defenseless, there's no visible trace of her strength. If a fly bothered her she wouldn't be able to flick it away, she couldn't scratch an itch. Here she is, and isn't. She lies suspended on this uncertain frontier.

"I'll go see Vincenzo this afternoon, I know he's fine," I tell her. "Papa's outside, and Piero."

Just then her eyes move, only reflexes.

Again there's a drip from the corner of her mouth, the nurse has gone. I use the clean sleeve of the smock I'm wearing, certainly Adriana is happier if I dry it.

"I wanted to call you Sunday, but then it was late," I tell her.

Maybe my voice a few hours earlier on the telephone could have infused more strength into the grip of her hand on the parapet, maybe she would have felt more solid, less alone.

I feel some guilt toward her. From a distance it was easy to abandon her to herself. I diminished the frequency of the calls, slowly unburdened myself of the weight of her life. She was an adult, a mother. I didn't want to be my sister's caretaker anymore.

"I'll wait until you recover, I won't leave," I reassure her now.

What I've constructed on the other side of the Alps suddenly appears small, poor, less important than the napkin that Adriana might have followed into the wind. Career, publications, exams. Established friendships and new ones, habits. I would exchange all my books for her reawakening, her health. I would burn them—my only patrimony—in Place Grenette if it were necessary, if the God I don't believe in would accept that sacrifice.

I don't pray, but I swear I'll give up everything, if it would help. I'll come back and live here, we'll open a restaurant together at the Dogana, as she's dreamed of for years. Or I'll help her fry fish along the shore, I'll hand the paper containers to the customers. It's my vow, my expiation.

We'll bump elbows in the narrow space of the Iveco, and today, this atrocious day that she can't see, will have been only one of the many of our lives.

Her neighbors were questioned, Piero said. Few were at home, at that hour the men were at sea, the children at school, and some women had already gone out shopping. The neighbor opposite Adriana is old and deaf, the one downstairs had the television on. No one knows anything. The voice that called 118 remains anonymous.

"The emergency workers were fast, in that she was lucky," the doctor said earlier.

He couldn't assure me that she will live. When I asked him

a second time he raised his bushy eyebrows and closed the file,
it didn't seem a good sign.

"Now go see her," and he took leave of me.

He is used to the death of his patients, I can't conceive of it
for Adriana. That's the difference. I'll stay until the last minute
of the two-hour visit without taking a step toward that possi-
bility. I don't want to prepare myself.

"This summer we'll go on a cruise."

We've been saying it for years, a plan that comes to nothing
every time because of my lack of commitment. She'd prefer the
Caribbean, I the Norwegian fjords, if anything. Our last vacations together go back to camping, free and wild, in borrowed
tents. We went hitchhiking, our parents didn't know where we
were going. They lacked the very idea of vacation: our father
stopped working only when the kiln left him unemployed, and
our mother's work in the house wasn't considered worthy of
rest or relaxation.

Adriana was quick to plant the stakes, unroll the sleeping
bags. In Umbria, near Spello. In the Gargano, where she nearly
drowned in a small cove.

"You were saved there, too," I remind her.

We tried to get what other girls had.

If our mother were here, she would kneel before the portrait of San Gabriele and the lilies, would ask for grace. I see
her, murmuring fervently: "Dear San Gabriele, you've taken
one, you have to leave me this one."

When she needed something she would suddenly populate
a whole sky with saints and Madonnas, as a girl I pitied her for
that. I already had a different faith, at night in bed I consumed
the pages of *Wuthering Heights*.

Adriana isn't exactly an atheist, but like many she doesn't
waste time. Feeding the divine in herself, taking part in rites.
But she insisted on the sacraments for her son, up to christen-
ing. I couldn't be the godmother, because of the divorce.

The lines seem regular, the numbers on the monitor hardly vary. That must be the pressure, it oscillates around 110/70. All this pain remains blind and without purpose, we don't know to whom we can offer it. No God stands over us or loves us.

In this anomalous intimacy, with the background of the assisted breathing, the sad, subdued whispering of the other families, I no longer know what to say to her, my work at the university bores her.

"You know I don't understand these things," she says when I try to tell her about it.

Then I tell her about the cat who gets fatter and fatter and sharpens his claws on the new carpet. Sometimes he scrapes away the dirt in the pots on the landing. Usually Christophe takes care of cleaning it up.

"At least you and your neighbor should get up to something, or is there no hope?" Adriana would ask at this point and I would call her an idiot.

Two beds away an alarm goes off, the *bleep bleep* becomes continuous and high-pitched, the corresponding wave flattens. A doctor and the nurses rush over. Arrest, says one, and immediately starts a cardiac massage. Adrenaline, the doctor asks for. Lori arranges some screens around the bed, invites all the family members to leave. I let go of Adriana's arm, I was squeezing it too tight, out of fear. In front of me walks the anguished relative of the person in arrest. She stops and leans on the wall of the corridor, she seems about to faint.

"Call a nurse," I say, and I hold her up.

Relief assails me, a mute, fierce joy: it didn't happen to my sister, it didn't happen to me.

20.

They won't let us go in again, visiting hours are almost over, my father says goodbye reluctantly and goes. He'll be back tomorrow, not tonight, he doesn't drive with the dark and the blinding headlights anymore. I take my time getting ready, along with the other relatives, we have a hard time leaving here. Piero follows me along the corridor, a man is walking quickly in the opposite direction, we look at each other for a moment. His face seems familiar, and also his gait, maybe he resembles someone I know. He lights up when we pass each other, he touches my arm, gentle but intense. He seems to want to stop, talk, instead he keeps going, transported by the automatic motion of his legs. I realize too late, I turn and no longer see him. He must already be in the waiting room for intensive care, they'll be telling him he can't go in. He also came for Adriana. That's who he resembles, the memory of the boy he was. We're all so changed.

Piero insists, I'll collapse if I don't have something to eat. At my every refusal his proposals are reduced: restaurant, snack bar, pizza at the hospital coffee shop.

"I'll eat later," I assure him.

I ask him to take me to Borgo Sud again. He pulls up where I tell him to and touches my hair with a gesture that was habitual, when we were together. His hand must have preserved the memory.

"Call me when you're ready, I'll come and get you."

I smile at him but won't call him. He drives off slowly. I'm alone in this place that doesn't belong to me but occasionally intersects with my life. Adriana brings me here. It seems to me that the sky is clearer and the air always has a scent of sea and garlic.

"Who are you?" asks the child who has opened the door only a little.

From inside voices and television, the damp warmth of a large family, the smell of lunch just eaten. Fish, certainly, I smell it even on the child who is looking at me with dark impatient eyes.

"I'm Vincenzo's aunt," I tell him.

Then he opens wider and Rosita is right behind him. She's drying her hands on her apron and hugs me tight. We separate to look at each other. Of the girl who had the market stall only the curls remain, and a distant flash in her pupils. She has five children, over the years Adriana has updated me on her pregnancies. She is moved for a moment, then she smiles faintly, showing the black line between crowns and gums. They're all silenced in the kitchen, only the cartoons are still chattering.

"Claudio persuaded him, they went to a field near Francavilla for a game. But they'll be back soon," Rosita says.

It was her voice on the phone that summoned me to Italy. My nephew is a year older than her oldest, they've grown up together here in Borgo, like their fathers.

I sit down at one end of the long lunch table, the tablecloth is still on it, with bits of bread and apple peel. Two girls approach, curious, I make an effort to be interested in them and immediately forget their names.

"You haven't eaten," Rosita guesses, and turns to the stove to heat up something, ignoring my protests.

"And Vincenzo?" I ask.

"Today yes, he liked it. Yesterday his stomach was still closed, nothing went down."

They told him that his mother isn't so serious, but they doubt that he believed it. I take off my jacket and am about to hang it on the back of the chair, the pigtailed girl takes it and puts it somewhere. She returns immediately to examine the details of how I'm dressed. She squats under the table, observes the pointy ankle boots with laces and a low spindle heel. Then she comes back up.

"You're wearing the Befana's shoes, but they're pretty," and she touches the sleeve of my shirt.

Rosita puts a steaming plate in front of me, it's just a couple of rigatoni, she insists, Antonio brought a kilo of calamari and she made a simple sauce.

I begin out of politeness, then I eat eagerly. The child looks at me, satisfied, the other is wrangling with her brothers, behind me. She calls her for help.

"Where is he?" I ask.

"At sea," and she's silent a moment. "With all these children to bring up I have to do something, too, in the morning I clean the stairs in some apartment buildings."

I drink a glass of water, she puts the coffeepot on the stove.

"Today Vincenzo went back to school. We didn't force him, he decided himself."

After dinner he wants to go home, Claudio goes with him, spends the night with him. At breakfast they're sitting at this table. Adriana fell from the terrace a few dozen meters from here, as the crow flies.

Rosita asks about her now. How did I find her, does she give any sign? No. She's sleeping. Sometimes she moves her eyes, but involuntarily. A hesitation, and then: is she in one piece?

I continue not to understand how she fell, I ponder aloud. She's distracted, yes, but really. Rosita takes away plate, fork, and glass, throws away the apple peels. In silence she removes the tablecloth and shakes the crumbs out the window. The pot on the stove gurgles, spreading the scent of coffee. The girl with the pigtails comes and complains: her brothers are playing on the Wii and she can't watch Pokémon on TV.

"Take it to the lady," the mother tells her, and she comes toward me with small steps, careful to hold the cup balanced.

"Now you and your sister go tidy up your room. You two," Rosita raises her voice speaking to the boys, "go and do your homework."

She sits at the other end of the table, opposite me, pours herself some coffee. It must be her place, with the stove and the sink within reach. "So you weren't here in Borgo when it happened?"

"I told you, I go and clean stairs in the mornings," she responds abruptly.

"And no one told you anything?"

There is a sudden reticence in the way she has of moving her head back and forth. She takes a sip and looks at me.

"And yet someone called 118," I say. "Strange he didn't wait with her for the ambulance."

Rosita opens her mouth, reflects for a moment, gives it up. She's conflicted. Then she bursts out.

"The people here mind their own business when fights are involved."

"Fights?" I repeat.

"We all heard them screeching like seagulls, and sometimes they'd also hit each other." She drinks her coffee in a gulp, with a sucking sound.

She gets up suddenly and threatens the boys she'll take away the Wii for a month. They turn it off, go noisily to their room. I remained with what she was saying a few moments before: they'd also hit each other.

"But who, Rosita, who?"

"You still don't get it? Adriana and Rafael."

But what reason is there to fight, I protest, they left each other years ago, they live in different places. Only Vincenzo binds them.

"What do you know in France? She even cleans his house every so often."

She sits back heavily, rests her roughened hands on the table. She looks at me patiently.

"Only that your sister talks too much and suddenly war breaks out, but don't think that she loses, eh. She gives it to him," and she beats the air with her right hand.

I choose my words carefully.

"Why are you talking to me about that? Does it have to do with Adriana's fall?"

She sighs and turns her head sideways. She stares for a long time at the refrigerator, where her children have attached magnets and stickers of all kinds, many of Pescara. Rosita reviews them one by one, while my heart is bombarding my temples.

"They heard yelling, first."

I can't find my voice for other questions. She wouldn't answer, anyway; she compresses her lips stubbornly, conclusively. We sit there, silent, the multiplied length of the table divides us. In the background the quiet hum of the refrigerator.

A din in one of the rooms, filtered through the closed door. Rosita stands, rolls up her sleeves. She looks at me questioningly.

"Don't worry about me," I say. "I'm going to get some air, I'll wait for Vincenzo outside."

The child with the pigtails reappears, carrying the jacket over her arms as if it were precious. She observes me as I put it on and seems satisfied with the final effect.

Outside I breathe deeply, the temperature's gone down. The sound of my heels on the pavement comforts me, I'm standing, moving. I reach the square, a bench, the metal chills my back and legs in strips. The mowed green, the last flowerings before winter. When the city redeveloped the area every family got a garden plot, Adriana explained to me last summer. She showed me the circle carved into the pavement, the symbol of Borgo, the fishing community.

Staying within the circle is strength, life and its meaning. Going outside it is to get lost, mixed up, head for a fight in other neighborhoods. It's not worth it, there's already danger in the sea, every day. From here you can't see it, but, beyond the irregular rows of houses, it's cold and dark now. It's the master of everyone here, the place of toil. It's luck and death.

For Adriana it's as if she'd been born in Borgo. I suggested sometimes that she should move to a more comfortable apartment, with an elevator, closer to Vincenzo's school.

"I'll help you with the rent," I offered.

"You don't understand," she said shaking her head. "What we have here isn't anywhere."

Her voice reverberates in me, slightly carried away.

I don't know when I lost her, where our intimacy was stranded. I can't trace it to a precise moment, a decisive episode, a quarrel. We only surrendered to distance, or maybe it was what we were secretly looking for: repose, shaking each other off.

She didn't tell me anything about the fights with Rafael. I knew they had separated, I didn't consider the aftermath. We're alike in that, incapable of truly separating from those we've loved.

If it's true that they hit each other, it was their way of staying connected. Rafael I don't even count, he left my affections many years ago. If it's true I'm ashamed of her, Adriana still has the bad habit of raising her hands. She uses them to go where she can't with words. She spared only her son and her sister, but her fury falls on us like a flaw, an original sin. It's written in our blood, it festers inside us, unexpressed.

I look around, in the already fading light of the short days. The trees, the empty benches of Piazza Rizzo, the windows through which you can see every movement. In place of a statue there's the boat Erminio Padre, repainted in white and blue, the triangular flags frayed by the wind. It's another fishermen's symbol. Now I'm sure they all know how Adriana fell, in this family so large and united even in silence.

"Danie', Danie'!" cries a voice from high up. With this Daniela, with the woman who's calling her and the others in Borgo, my sister went to the beach at dawn every June 24th. Together they bathed feet, hands, forehead, asking the sea and San Giovanni for strength, health, intelligence for a year. Last time the water dried too soon on Adriana's skin.

An old man passes and points at me, I'm a stranger to him. What am I doing here? Sitting where a century ago was a swamp. I wonder, too. I'm waiting for Vincenzo. I've been preparing for two days and now that he's coming I can no longer find the words.

21

I ring the bell of the green house, even though the door is half open. I haven't talked to Rafael for years, but I've seen him a few times. Adriana reluctantly described his ruin, one bit every summer. They had a brief happy period. I remember when he returned from Africa and the boat reappeared in its place, moored at the bollard. Then my sister helped him with the fishing, the only woman in Borgo who went to sea. On Sundays they walked in the city center, boldly. They thought they had life in their grasp, in those two hours.

During that time they got married. They paid off the debts, a little every month, and Isolina took care of Vincenzo. Her name, painted on the sides of the boat, burned on a moonless night in the port channel, along with the whole boat. An empty jerry-can of gas was found, never who had set the fire.

The crates are here and there on the ground, only some are still stacked. Maybe it's the wind or these skinny cats wandering around. They must have chosen one as a litter box, on the bottom are large bits of soft shit. From inside the house an out-of-tune guitar breaks off and starts again a few seconds later. He's trying to tune it. I press the bell again and wait. A white cat with red and black patches gets between my feet, encircles them, brushing me with her tail up to the knees. Now I hear the voice, too.

I go in, I don't know how many of them are coming toward me along the hall. I can't see them, I move slowly so as not to step on them. The stink of pee makes the air unbreathable.

"Rafael," I call, but he doesn't answer.

He's singing a sailor's song, inertly. He's nearly in the dark, sitting in the kitchen. I turn on the light. He blinks, widens his palm on the scratched guitar.

"Hello, madame," and he looks at me with rheumy eyes moving calmly up from my feet.

On his thigh a cat plays with the broken string, shoots it into the air. Two others seem like knick-knacks on the crocheted doily that was Isolina's. They stare at me from the table, still as sphinxes. The cigarette in the ashtray is smoked down almost to the filter.

"You're not well?" I ask Rafael.

The overall leaves his swollen, cyanotic ankles bare. He has nothing in common with the young man in military uniform getting dusty on a shelf.

"I'm fine. And how is it you deign to come to my house?"

"Vincenzo is worried about you, he says you won't open the door."

He starts tuning the guitar again, he turns the pegs and checks the sound every time. He seems to have forgotten about me.

"My son doesn't have to worry, he knows I'm getting a little deaf."

He takes the cat that's playing with the string off his stomach, places it delicately on the floor. Right away another one leaps from somewhere I can't see to occupy the free place on Rafael's legs. He caresses its back and speaks to it as to a small child.

"You were waiting your turn, eh?"

He changes his tone suddenly to speak to me.

"If you want to sit down, take that one," and he indicates a chair.

Its padding is coming out, you can see the foam rubber inside. I remain standing, nor do I take off my jacket, it's cold here.

"You know about Adriana, right?" I ask.

"I know she broke her head, yeah," and he beats his hand against the sound box.

The cats searching around the empty bowls turn to look at him and then start circling again.

"Your sister never pays attention," Rafael adds, accompanying himself with fingers on the strings. "I'm always telling her to pay attention, but she won't change her ways."

A din behind me distracts us, it's a movement in a bag leaning against the wall. "Salmon-flavored dry food" is written on it, vitality for your four-legged friends. It's a third full, a friend has gotten inside it and can't get out. It wriggles, meows, frightened. Rafael observes the jerks of the body imprisoned in the paper and laughs.

"That's how you'll learn to be so smart," he warns.

The cat flies out, finally, sated and shocked. The others look at him in bewilderment. I start to feel itchy on my neck, my legs. The floor is dirty, the sink loaded with encrusted dishes and pots. If it's true that my sister came now and then to clean, it's weeks since she was here. On a shelf a haphazard pile of tickets for scratch-and-win.

"You're not working?" I venture.

"It's all you think about, work, work. You feel strong because you have an important position, right?" He looks at my mouth waiting for the answer, immediately gets impatient and continues.

"But tomorrow the end of the world arrives and you lose it all in an instant. Then you find yourself worse off than me, I already know how it goes."

I remain silent, stricken. He continues on his own:

"In the middle of the sea I was a king, but then my crown fell off. On land I'm not good for anything."

I move to avoid a cat that is brushing hard against my boot. Its furless ears are covered with bleeding scabs.

"That one's got scabies, let's hope it doesn't infect the others. Your sister can't stand my kitties, she chases them out with the broom."

It's too many, I say, it's not healthy to live with all these animals. Also for Vincenzo when he comes.

"You're right, but what can I do if they have babies? At first there were only four."

He points with both hands to the hungry multitude. They move nervously, tails up. They walk around me.

"Would you get me a beer, please?" and he indicates the refrigerator.

I'm a little uncertain, then decide to move the few steps necessary, amid the furry bodies. They rush in as soon as I open it, they hiss, they scratch each other in the crush.

"Hey, hey, get out of there," Rafael shouts, and to me: "Give them a kick."

I grab the bottle and close it, some almost get shut inside. I glimpsed pieces of moldy cheese, empty cartons, rotten salad. Still some clawing among the cats, they calm down slowly. They remain alert for food.

I hand the beer to Rafael, he opens it with his teeth. Swallowing noisily he drinks almost half.

"You want some?" and he holds the bottle out toward me.

"So, that's enough. What happened to my sister?"

He puts the guitar on the floor, the cats get up on it.

"That's why she came to see Rafael, the madame. She wants to know what happened, but Rafael has nothing to do with it: he was here with all of you, right? We told the police."

The animals move in a wave, all in his direction, under the chair, behind, beside it. They stare at me, hostile, thick around the head. I'm afraid now, and he sniffs it, stronger than the stink he doesn't smell. He drinks again, caresses the one that sits on his shoulder like a valet, a secretary.

"Your sister got what she deserves. If she wakes up she'll

tell you she does it with the engineer, she brings him here to Borgo."

Again he's changed his tone, like an actor who's playing several parts.

"What do you mean? Who are you talking about?" I shout.

He gets up and grabs the bag, the cats press around him, meowing madly. He ignores the bowls, pours the food right on the floor, they'll clean it all up. He continues to speak to them, to call them pet names, easy, easy, he tells them, don't choke. I don't know what's keeping me here, at this spectacle of madness.

The rigatoni and calamari are rising in my stomach, I rouse myself. In a moment I reach the hall and turn on the light, I avoid the shit on the floor. Then I'm outside, I close the door behind me. I lean on a lamp post and breathe deeply, master the nausea. When I raise my head Vincenzo is there looking at me, pale under the tuft of black hair. I thought he was at Rosita's.

We walk toward the river now. He dictates the pace with his long thin legs.

"I didn't know your father was in those conditions."

"Papa's not bad, only he's let himself go a bit."

"What are all the boxes for he has in front of the house?" I ask.

He works for a big supermarket on the Tiburtina, Vincenzo begins. He loads fish at the port and delivers it. He should get rid of the empty containers, but he's piled up the last ones there. Sooner or later he'll throw them away, he assures me.

"He doesn't seem to be working," I observe.

Right now he doesn't feel very well, but he'll recover. He has to resolve a problem with his license.

"Was it taken away from him?" I ask.

No, it only expired. Vincenzo is evasive, or maybe he really doesn't know. A car speeds by, hands wave to him from the window.

"And the cats?"

"When you find them around how can you not feed them?"

"Well, you could just keep them outside," I say.

"So you're all mad at him? My mother, the neighbors, now you, too," Vincenzo bursts out. "What did he do to you, what do you want from Papa?"

I remind him that Adriana tries to clean that house, and is worried about Rafael.

"She's not worried, she judges him. Rather: she despises him. If she goes to clean she does it for me, not for him."

This isn't a walk. He strides with his fists sunk in the pockets of his uniform, an angry forward motion. I struggle to keep up. At sixteen he's already understood too much, and I don't know how to soften the reality.

"Your parents have a long history behind them. They were very united, but then something changed," and I touch his back.

"Now all they do is fight." He kicks an empty can.

"But you're the child of that time, of when they were happy."

I would like to talk to him about Adriana and me, of the sacred slightly twisted loves we found as young women. So different, and neither of the two destined to last. We kept them alive beyond their time. I would also like to tell him that by being born he saved his mother.

Instead I'm silent until the intersection and then I ask him how he's doing at school, if he's still so good in math.

"I got a ten on my homework, aunt, the prof never gives a ten." He slows down and looks at me.

"I knew it," and I squeeze his wrist. I bet on his future.

We turn onto Via Andrea Doria, a few steps away is the bus stop. Here it is arriving, the arrow is lighted. Vincenzo leans down to my height, hugs me suddenly, blinding me with the shampoo-perfumed hair.

"Say hello, I'll come when she wakes up."

22

I had gotten the job in Grenoble, I was getting ready to leave. Adriana arrived on the afternoon train, without the child.

"If I brought him we wouldn't get anything done," she said, but maybe she wanted to spend some time alone with me.

From the station she wanted to walk around the city: she'd never seen it. Macerata seemed small to her, she doubted there was a university.

"I've been teaching here for two years, I should know if it exists," I laughed. "It's very old and prestigious." And I pointed out to her the façade of Palazzo Ugolini.

"Then why are you leaving?" she asked.

I turned my back to her and headed toward home. The apartment was small, and bare. The only luxury was the double bed with a wrought-iron headboard, the owner's grandmother had slept in it. From Pescara I'd brought some clothes and shoes, the books I needed to prepare the classes.

"You certainly don't use the kitchen," Adriana guessed.

I seldom went home for lunch and at night I sometimes had just bread and tomatoes. She inspected the pantry, the nearly empty refrigerator.

"What do you live on?"

"I buy what I need," I said.

But I took her for dinner to Secondo, I wanted to celebrate her arrival. The antipasto fritto misto excited her, she ate the ascolane olives and cremini mushrooms eagerly. The waiter greeted some people who had reserved, among them a colleague in Modern History. He stopped, and I introduced Adriana. He was an attractive man and knew it. Even I realized it. He rested his hand with its perfect nails on the table, near mine.

"I'm still struggling to understand your decision. And what does Morelli say?" He drummed on the white tablecloth with his index finger, while my sister, watching, enjoyed herself.

My professor had been the first to know. We had met on a Sunday in a café in Pescara. No surprise at my decision, and he hadn't even tried to dissuade me, in fact he had been lavish with advice.

"It will be good for you," he had concluded.

We had embraced at the door, I remember the softness of his jacket and the usual modest but persistent scent. He hadn't been surprised, either, by the end of my marriage; we had talked about it other times. The separation was also good for me, I imagine, and yet he was sorry about it.

Adriana barely left time for my colleague to sit down at his table.

"And here's that guy, how is it that you're leaving?" she started again, winking.

"Here I'm not far enough away," I said. "And I think about it all the time."

She took a bite and drained her glass of verdicchio.

"About Piero?"

I looked for him without knowing it, during walks along the sea or in the center. One day I read his name on an office sign and didn't understand how I had gotten there. I started when I seemed to recognize him at a distance. Again that sensation of a bump or a ditch, more painful than before. Close up it was never Piero, the resemblance only in a detail that my desire had magnified. I returned to Pescara every other Saturday, just to take a chance on the unlikely probability of running into him.

"I let him go like that, overnight," I said, stirring the fork around on my plate.

I had stayed in Via Zara only a week longer than him. I hadn't even taken the wedding presents from my relatives with me, they must have ended up somewhere or other I don't know, along with the marriage. I had stayed with Michela in Chieti for a period, and every morning we went to the university together.

"You couldn't do anything," Adriana said, pouring herself some wine. "Piero isn't who you thought he was when you got married."

And yet I woke up every morning happy next to that unknown person.

"I have to get away, nothing changes here, it's like the first day."

"At least be careful that you don't take him with you."

I wanted to obey her, but Piero must have sneaked into the suitcase, escaping my control. He became an expatriate with me, an incurable habit.

That night Adriana and I slept in the double bed, talking about when we used to sleep together as children.

"This mattress is nice and big, then we had to do head to foot," she recalled. "You came from the city, precise as a doll, and I was wetting the bed."

It happened on alternating nights, and she seemed not to notice. She spread the wet sheets quickly in the tub and said nothing. I also pretended not to notice the wet bed. She told me in Macerata, after all those years, how ashamed she was.

In the morning we packed the bags and cleaned the house. We put the books in big boxes to send to Grenoble. With a skeptical expression Adriana turned over in her hands Garboli's *Secret Game*, which she had found open on the desk.

We divided the jobs, I the kitchen, she the bathroom. Every so often we called to each other. I heard her scrubbing with the sponge and the rag, cursing an obstinate stain on the mirror.

That won't go away, I called with my head in the oven. Around eleven she came to make another coffee, we drank it standing up. Just what we needed, she said. Then she turned on the radio, went back to work. When she finished, the fixtures and taps shone.

Piero, on the other hand, had emptied our house slowly. He came one afternoon to take away the remains of his life there. First a racquet in its case and some issues of the magazine *Matchball*, with a champion on every red cover. Afterward he opened the sliding door of the closet and a suitcase, took the last clothes off the hangers. He folded them on the bed, his hands slightly unsteady.

Leaning against the doorframe I watched him. He hesitated at a linen shirt I'd given him a few months earlier, lingered over the fabric with his fingers. He put it in, on top of a sweater. He turned toward me, to beg me yet again to stay in the apartment. In the house his father had bought—not if I were dead, I said to him. He insisted it was our house, mine. I shouldn't have to face the discomfort of moving.

"Now you're worried about my discomfort," I shouted at him.

He who had always lied to me, who had pretended love but wanted another, others. He who had deceived me at every moment of every day of our years together. I shouted like that, until my throat was raw, the root of my tongue. How much he had forced himself to please me in that bed and how I had disgusted him, yes, disgusted, I repeated while he shook his head no. I slid my back down the doorframe, I found myself sitting on the floor with tears pouring out, mucus from my nose. He leaned over me, caressed my hair.

"I didn't force myself and I never pretended with you. I told some lies, that's true."

He had drawn me into his confusion. My accusations weakened.

"I didn't do it on purpose," he defended himself.

"You couldn't understand it before?" I repeated, my voice breaking.

He rested one knee on the floor. He took my hands and held them together, all four, he kissed mine, which resisted furiously. It lasted a moment, I freed myself.

I could also hate him, he said, but he would continue to love me even against my will. It was his last promise and I think that, essentially, he kept it. On the tracks of that unyielding love I returned to Pescara every other Saturday. I can still smell him in the places where I was with him. Our faithfulness is so intangible.

He got up, I heard him zip the zipper, carry the suitcase and the rest into the hall, to the front door and the landing. The elevator came up, opened. I knew all the sounds by heart. It descended with him.

I punched the floor between my legs, then I jumped up and ran to a window that looked onto the street. From the invisible sky a thick vertical rain fell. Piero went out the front door, carrying his things, he had parked right in front. He put them in the trunk, the racquet, protected by its case, last. He was about to get in the car and disappear. Recalled by my gaze, he looked up toward our floor. He took off his cap and stood defenseless in the rain. I rested my hands against the glass and I don't know how long we stayed like that, he with the rain pasting his hair to his forehead, running down his face. He left, my fingers squeaked along the glass.

I think the apartment was sold quickly. It wasn't difficult in that location, with the view of the sea.

Her second night in Macerata Adriana sat next to me on the green couch, poked me with her elbow.

"Have some fun in France, if you've got your head in the books night and day you'll never forget him," she said.

We ate pizza, taking the slices directly from the box.

"That way we won't get even a fork dirty," she had laughed.

After the end of my marriage I went from the university to Michela's house and vice versa, with rare variations. I didn't go out with her into the streets for the Chieti evening stroll. Even then I liked to listen to the students at the end of my classes, as they got ready to leave the room. I overheard their hopes, the push toward the future. They were in a hurry to graduate, win competitions, be happy. I would have liked to say, Just a moment, kids, the lesson begins now. You're deceiving yourselves. An accident will happen, sickness, an earthquake, and your dreams will be cut off. You'll get lost.

I kept silent, slowly put on my jacket. A tenderness invaded me, they were so young, they didn't deserve the truth. Who was I, to tell it to them. Maybe fate would spare them.

That night Adriana and I talked until late. Last she reported some gossip about a classmate of hers.

"Her lover told half the town that she does certain jobs with her mouth," she said.

She imitated the face of the husband when he found out, exaggerating the expressions. We were seized by an uncontrollable laughter, like girls. Our bodies remembered the small bed of that time, we hugged each other in our sleep, our hair got tangled.

In the morning I let her sleep. Her train left at noon, mine at eight. We didn't say goodbye, I preferred it that way. She was snoring, her head disheveled and one foot sticking out of the sheets. I left a note telling her to turn off the gas and put the key on the table, the landlady would come by to get it. As a paperweight I used a rubber whale, it was for Vincenzo.

I had a heavy suitcase, a backpack, and an over-the-shoulder purse: I called a taxi, for once. In the brief ride to the station I checked the train tickets, the times of the changes at Civitanova Marche, Bologna, and Turin. I would think about the change at Chambéry after crossing the border. A long journey awaited me.

23.

I go to see her every day, during the hours allowed. Even with a place like that you come to terms, find a familiarity. My sister sleeps and changes, her bruises veer from blue to purple and greenish. They shift through gravity, are very slowly reabsorbed.

I walk along the sea after leaving her. I change the air in my lungs, and my thoughts, too, lighten. The seagulls perched on a wall look at me with a single eye.

I haven't gone to dinner with Piero and now he's stopped insisting. He comes to get me every so often at the hospital, in front of the hotel I say bye and get out. It seems to me that for him that invitation remains outstanding.

Many years have passed since then. Sometimes I was gripped by a suspicion that I had estranged him, that I had pushed him in a direction away from my body. It didn't take much to feel that the fault was mine.

Now it's not hard to give up seeing him. I take small doses, I protect the equilibrium I've found. This, today, is my choice.

Adriana has been through some crises, hypotension. In yesterday's conversation the doctor with the geometric beard talked about a complicated night, about convulsive episodes, and I was afraid to ask more. Every morning a physiotherapist massages her and moves her limbs, as much as possible. Meanwhile she sleeps, under the influence of Versed and Propofol. Of flexings and extensions, of the weather outside, of the world and herself she knows nothing.

That doctor is blunt and direct in communicating the news. He protects himself, the families of the patients say in the waiting room, so if it goes wrong you can't complain. Yesterday, to my surprise, he asked me if there had been other suicide attempts. She's not that kind of person, I answered, but he wasn't satisfied. Then how did she fall off a terrace? Hanging up laundry, I said sharply. I chased away the face of Rafael that flashed before me for a second. And didn't I find it strange? the doctor insisted, clicking the pen. And didn't he find it strange that she had hung the sheets on the line a moment before jumping? Accidents happen. It wasn't curiosity, he just wanted me to consider the psychological aspect of the future rehabilitation. Click, clack. Assuming everything is all right. Click, clack. After the neurosurgeon the orthopedic surgeon also operated, put an intramedullary rod in the diaphyseal femur fracture. Click, clack. Even in the best of hypotheses she won't be scampering home, the recovery will be slow and gradual, she'll need therapy and help. He put down the pen and answered the question he read in my eyes. At least a year.

I didn't think I would stay so long. I had thought till Christmas, at most early January. I had imagined returning to Grenoble after the winter break, the snow on the campus lawns. Only a few days ago I swore to myself I'd give up everything in exchange for Adriana's life, and now I'm not ready to sacrifice a year to her. My resolutions are so frail.

In these weeks I've stopped thinking about the conference on Italian women writers of the nineteenth and twentieth centuries. It's scheduled for March, I still don't know whether to put it off. Some colleagues have already confirmed their talks, Martin-Gistucci would give a preview of her new monograph on Matilde Serao. Maybe I could leave Adriana for a short time, when she's better. They'd help her in Borgo and she can count on Vittorio.

The evening of my first day here we met in the waiting room.

"You didn't recognize me in the corridor today," he said.

I held out my hand but he hugged me, emotional.

"Can I talk to you afterward?" I asked.

We divided the visiting hours in half. When he came out of the ward and sat for a moment to recover, I waited for him. We went out together, following the colored stripes. I asked him about his work. He's managing the construction of generators at Collarmele, which with this expansion will become one of the most important wind parks in Italy, he said in a moment of pride. I know where it is, the bare mountain with a view over the landscape of Silone.

Vittorio suggested an aperitivo in a bar on the street. We had no wish to drink, but it was quiet at the table in the corner.

"What do you think happened on that terrace?"

It was a question I could no longer hold back.

"Only she could tell us," Vittorio answered, looking out.

He was silent for a moment while the waiter served us tonic water. Then he began to circle around some suspicions, wary at first. That she wasn't alone up there. That someone had joined her, sure of finding her there. In Borgo everyone's habits are known, and, besides, Adriana sings when she hangs out the laundry. Maybe someone went up the stairs, drawn by her voice in the morning. He must have rung a bell, or taken advantage of someone going out. And no one speaks, in the building no one saw anything. But among themselves they whisper of shouted insults, of a very loud cry and the final blow. If there hadn't been the awning on the second floor Adriana would have been dead on impact.

"Rafael?" I asked.

He just nodded, his mouth twisted bitterly. That's why they won't speak, he's someone from the place, and the people of

Borgo won't interfere between man and woman. They separated years ago, I objected. Never truly, he said, raising his glass. Adriana cleaned Rafael's house, he's the father of my child, she explained. Vincenzo shouldn't find that filth, she said, fighting the cats.

There were more violent fights, the last time because he stole the money from her wallet. She realized it at the supermarket checkout, and went back to confront him, burning with rage. Maybe she didn't expect that reaction, from someone so weak.

"She was all bruised, but she refused to report him. Only she promised not to see him anymore."

It lasted a few weeks, then she returned to the green house with some excuse. She wasn't afraid of a wimp, she said. Or that fear, which she'd always known, was necessary to her.

The ice cubes melted slowly in the glass, Vittorio had drunk only a swallow. With the spoon he stirred the peanuts in the bowl, but didn't eat any. He was thinking of her and was very tired.

"They asked if I'm her husband, on the ward."

He said yes, otherwise they wouldn't have let him enter.

"Then who are you for Adriana?"

They've been spending more time together, he said evasively. They meet at his house, in the city center, sometimes they go to the movies or the beach.

In the past few months she's invited him to lunch on a Sunday now and then. Maybe Rafael saw him, or someone told him. What was tolerable from a distance he couldn't stand in Borgo, where the gossip flew from mouth to mouth. Maybe ours are fantasies, I said.

"Yes, but look at your sister's bruises. They're not all compatible with the fall."

"What do you mean?"

"You can see marks on her hands."

He's angry with Adriana, who won't listen to him. She's never listened to anyone, for that matter, but I keep it to myself. She's impetuous, she lives in disorder. She keeps this man on a string, gives him a little more and then avoids him, the same game as always. Some afternoons she spends hours with him, but she's not in love. Then she goes to her van. The normality he offers frightens her, she sees death in it.

That night Vittorio drove me to the hotel. Adriana was so present in the car I could hear her mechanical breathing.

A funny puppet hung from the rearview mirror, I caught it in one of its oscillations. He turned toward me and smiled for a moment, and nodded as if I had asked him. That soft cheerful owl was a gift from Adriana.

The night clerk was already on duty, he placed my key on the counter as I approached.

"Have you decided how long you're staying? So I'll note it," he said.

I took the key and was silent, searching for an answer.

"It depends on how long my commitments in Pescara are extended, I don't know precisely," I hedged.

But he had to write something on the reservation he insisted, polite but firm. He must have been the owner, from the way he behaved. I suddenly hated him, him and his hotel, the rigid writing on the page of the register. The metal was sweating in my hand.

"Then write that my sister is in a coma and I don't know if she'll die or wake up, or when," and I left him with an expression of astonishment.

I was already ashamed going up in the elevator and would have liked to apologize, not to him but to Adriana. It was the first time I'd named her death. I was afraid of having summoned it.

I sat on the bed, shivering without my jacket. A hint of winter had entered the room with me, the cold of November. A scarf was hanging on the chair and I wrapped it around my neck.

I carried in my ears the echo of Vittorio's words. I no longer knew Adriana, I don't recognize her. From a distance I thought I'd kept her with me, and it was only an old idea of her, of when we were young, with our dreams still intact. She wanted to open that fish restaurant on Via Andrea Doria, near the Dogana. Rafael would dock the boat right in front, unloading the boxes with the dying shrimp.

I returned every summer, for Christmas vacation, and I saw nothing. It was a time too short to pick up the truth about my sister. We told each other the best of our lives, as people do when they're distant.

She worked when she could, she brought up Vincenzo. I was satisfied with that. I don't know how she and Rafael had reached that point, that she went with him to his ruin.

The day of my wedding she adjusted my train when I entered the church, he was waiting for her in the first row and had kept a place for her. Our parents didn't know that we had invited him, but for once they had no reproach. He was handsome, his curls tamed by gel, his skin tanned on the boat, his eyes black and shiny. Adriana sat next to him and he took her hand. He admired her, dressed in red. Every so often I glanced at them while the priest officiated and Piero held his palm between my shoulder blades. A cabbage butterfly flew up to the altar, rested on the linen cloth and on some of the white roses. We were all so happy that day.

24

She opens her eyes, she sees him. She doesn't know who it is, that face, she doesn't recognize the place. The dose of Versed is at the minimum, consciousness returns to the surface. Something scrapes between tongue and throat, an alien body that has been there for two weeks. The hand would tear it away, but it doesn't respond to commands yet.

She coughs, she's agitated. In the violent light the anesthesiologist speaks calmly, tells her where she is and a few other facts. He calls her by name, she hears him amazed.

It's eight in the morning and she's almost weaned from the ventilator, the saturation of oxygen in the blood wavers between 95 and 100. The machine is turned off, we can proceed.

"Now we'll take this annoyance out of your mouth," the doctor tells her.

He says the words clearly in order to be understood. The nurse is beside him, it's Lori's shift.

"Hold still now," she urges and smiles at her while she aspirates the tracheobronchial secretions with a sticky suction.

Two weeks of treatments converge in a single moment: the anesthesiologist capsizes the security bubble, takes out Adriana's tubes.

She's free. Stunned, her eyes wide. The first breaths, as when she was born, but now she's not crying. The involuntary contraction of the diaphragm isn't enough for her, it takes the force of the major and minor pectorals, the accessory muscles.

She lifts ribs and sternum as much as she can, under negative pressure the air erupts furiously, fills her lungs. Adriana feels the breath on her mucous membranes, it goes in and out, in and out. No longer enhanced or aseptic, it's the impure air of the world. From now on she'll have to defend herself on her own: dust, virus, bacteria fluctuate in suspension. And all the pain she still can't see, sedated in the other beds.

"Slowly, slowly, just think about breathing," says the doctor and mimes the movements holding his palm against his chest. She looks at him, has confidence. She slows down, repeats fifteen times a minute the act necessary to stay among the living. She learns it from the beginning, at the start of her middle age. Every so often she coughs.

Sometimes in the hours that follow she falls asleep, and every time she wakes is disoriented. She wavers between being there and not being there. Someone keeps a constant watch, but she manages to detach an electrode from her skin, then the central venous catheter. A concert of alarms is set off and blood gushes out.

At that very moment I'm on a bench trying to read the paper I bought, but worry about her distracts me. Maybe she's found herself naked and alone in strange hands, with the sleepers all around. Who knows how much she remembers of herself.

I imagine what's happening, I lose my place in the article and give it up. I'm waiting to see her and the wait has never been so long.

I write to Christophe that I'm still in Italy, Hector is in his care. His answer makes the phone in my purse vibrate immediately: I shouldn't worry, I'll make up for it on my return. I remind him also to water the orchids I keep on the windowsill. Before departing I left him the key in the mailbox. He hasn't forgotten, he writes. Exclamation points follow and kisses. He must be at the computer, with his glasses a little crooked. I smile at him from here.

Meanwhile Lori has washed her face and hair, dried it with the dryer. She ties the ponytail using a new elastic net.

"We have to straighten ourselves," she tells her, "your sister will be here soon."

I find her sitting up in bed. I thought I was prepared but her gaze melts every resistance. I hug her like a fragile body, suddenly I understand that I almost lost her. They've put on a hospital gown with geometric designs and I cry on it. That's how I celebrate her life.

"Why am I in the hospital?" she protests.

"You fell, you don't remember?"

"O.K., but now I'm going home," and she lifts up the sheet.

She's curious about her skinny legs, she observes the plaster and the still fresh wound on the other thigh. She runs her index finger over the points of the sutures, then she tries to move to get down and a cry escapes. She's still too weak, I tell her she has to have patience.

"They operated on your femur, you'll need rehab."

She looks at me frightened.

"I'll be there to help you. I'll take you to the sessions, I won't leave," and I hold her hand, light again after the days when it was heavy and inert.

"Did you take in the clothes I hung out?" she asks as if it had happened a few hours ago.

"Yes, I even folded them and put them away."

She closes her eyes and nods several times before sleep takes her again. It lasts a few minutes, she awakens apprehensive.

"Now Vincenzo's coming home from school and I haven't cooked."

"Today he'll have lunch at Rosita's and tonight he'll come and see you," I reassure her. "You can be calm, he's grown up now, and he can even manage by himself."

"What do you know about it?" she says, promptly.

Anything that has to do with children I can't understand,

it's the usual story and it doesn't even hurt me anymore. I don't regret the children I didn't have. Sometimes I miss them, but I never really wanted them. I could exist without.

We're silent for a while, at this reunion so different from other times.

"If I died would you cry?" she asks then.

"Of course, but what sort of conversation is this?"

"At Mamma's funeral you didn't shed a tear, that's why I'm asking."

What does she know, she came late, I remind her after all these years.

"It was clear from your face," she says, certain.

She tries to turn onto one side, curls herself into her favorite sleeping position. She moves cautiously, no alarm sounds.

"Now when you leave go to Borgo, to the parish of Gesù Maestro, and say a prayer."

"What prayer?"

"One you have in mind. For me and Vincenzo, and also for you, you might need it."

I'd like to ask more but she's not listening to me anymore.

"If you see Don Giorgio say hello for me," and already the voice is coming from the darkness.

I look at her for a moment, in the almost natural sleep. Visiting hours are over and the relatives are moving away from the beds, turning into the corridor. Today my step is light on the linoleum.

I have all afternoon ahead of me and I'm not hungry. I walk toward Borgo, pondering my sister's request. In the line of cars at the red light a schoolgirl with blond braids waves with her hand on the glass.

A prayer, Adriana wants, and I don't know any. As a child yes, all by heart. I haven't exactly forgotten them but if I try to whisper one it sounds fake. Like making the sign of the cross when I enter a church just to see it. I stopped believing so

many years ago. And yet even in my mouth a mysterious gratitude for this salvation is growing.

On the bridge a scooter without a muffler passes and deaf-
ens me, I wait for the noise to get lost zigzagging in the traffic.
In the distance is the other bridge, the Ponte del Mare, with its
cables, suspended over the sweet and salt water of the river's
mouth. Not far away is the Ferris wheel. I'd like to go there
with Adriana, when she can. Already I hear her shouts at the
highest point, her laughter.

Her leg worries me, I talked about it yesterday with the
orthopedist. The problem is the femoral nerve, he said, we'll
have to see what she recovers in the next months. I can't imagine her limping, that must be what I have to pray for. And so
that my mother's curse on a long-ago afternoon will be lifted.

I've seen the parish church she mentioned in Borgo, it's on
the ground floor of an apartment building and the door opens
onto the square. It has vent-like windows and the neon sign is
always lighted, the fishermen can see it when they leave home
in the dark to go to their boats.

I'm going in the afternoon. In a little while I'll sit in an
empty pew and make my wishes for Adriana's future. That the
marriage made secretly one Sunday in May at Punta Penna, in
the church by the sea, will be dissolved. She told me months
later, the witnesses had been Rosita and Antonio. This time I'll
go with her, to a lawyer.

As for me, I'll wait patiently to return to Grenoble. I miss
the air of the valley floor and the dampness of the two rivers,
even the dusty haze. I miss the view of the mountains from the
city streets.

I know what to ask for, not from whom. The November sky
is clear and empty. Only the eternal laws that rule the movement of the stars and the cycles of the seasons on Earth will
bring luck to Vincenzo, and maybe some peace to my sister.
That's the only prayer.

A special thanks to the women and men of Borgo Marino in Pescara.